Settling Down

By

Cadee Brystal

Settling Down

By Cadee Brystal

ISBN-10: 0991441745
ISBN-13: 978-0-9914417-4-7

Dear Reader,

Thank you for choosing to return to Miller's Bend for the third installment in the Lessons of Love series! You will find yourself rooting for Ashley and Matt as they learn to be patient and trust in each other.

As in *Wide Open Spaces* and *Breaking Free*, you will find characters who are down to earth and genuine. They are neither billionaires nor superstars. They could be your neighbors or your friends. They are imperfect works in progress.

Join Matt as he learns that he can let go of trying to control everything and being responsible for all those he loves. He also learns that some of the lessons life taught him when he was younger were wrong.

Ashley is surprised to learn that her fast-paced life isn't as fulfilling as it once was. With the help of her friends, she learns the joys of living small and loving fully.

Be sure to watch for clues about the fourth book in the series.

Happy reading!
Cadee Brystal

THANK YOU

Thank you to my readers who embraced the characters in *Wide Open Spaces* and *Breaking Free*. I'm so glad you enjoy my stories, and that you are looking forward to following Matt and Ashley as they begin to learn the lessons of love in Miller's Bend.

Thank you to all my friends and family members who have supported me and encouraged me to share the stories with you.

Special thanks to my volunteer collaborators, Jessica, Marlys, Terri, Jenny, Tammie, Char and MaKayla. And to my husband for his ongoing love, support and advice.

Cadee Brystal

Miller's Bend Series

By Cadee Brystal

Wide Open Spaces

Breaking Free

Settling Down

Taking Care

“DON’T PRAY FOR PATIENCE.”

One of Cadee’s former employers used to advise her to pray for patience. She later learned that when one prays for patience, God doesn’t give you patience, He gives you the opportunities to develop patience.

Getting Matt and Ashley’s story into print has been an opportunity in developing patience. This story was more challenging for Cadee and the steps necessary to get it into the hands of you, the reader, have taken a round-about path. But at last, here it is!

Cadee has continued to create characters who are down to earth in her contemporary Christian romance stories. “It is important that my readers be confident that the books indeed meet the criteria for Christian fiction,” she said. The novels are engaging with suspenseful storylines and unexpected twists. Her books continue to deliver messages of Christian faith applicable in our contemporary lives.

Important warning for readers sensitive to violence: You may wish to skip over Chapter 17, which begins on page 201. The chapter depicts a scene that wouldn’t be questioned in mainstream works, but in the world of flinch-free fiction, may be too graphic for some readers. If you skip over it, you will have no problem picking up the flow of the story in Chapter 18.

CONTENTS

CHAPTER ONE

She hadn't meant to overhear. She hadn't wanted to witness the unfolding drama. Ashley had only wanted to be alone for a while when she slipped out of the reception hall. Now she leaned against the rough brick wall in the shadows, wondering if she should make her presence known.

Sounds of joyful celebration drifted out of the building reminding her of the overwhelmingly happy bride and groom who danced away the evening inside. Festive music and laughter filled the air. Happiness. It seemed that the entire little town of Miller's Bend was awash in happiness. Everyone that is, with the exception of the couple who had invaded her solitude.

The man was tall and lean. His light blond hair and crystal blue eyes had Ashley trying to guess whether he was descended from the Nordic or from the Dutch. He'd been the usher who seated her just moments before the ceremony in which one of Ashley's best friends had married. She didn't know his name or a thing about him, but her heart went out to him. Judging by the body language and other clues she was picking up, the shapely strawberry-blonde he'd been dancing with all night was about to cut him loose.

As if she were watching a muted TV show, Ashley made up the dialogue for the couple.

She: “I don’t want to see you anymore.”

He: “Please, don’t leave me.”

She: “This isn’t working.”

He: “I’ll do anything. Just don’t go.”

She: “I’ve met someone else.”

He: “Someone else? I don’t understand.”

She: “Don’t be naïve. Of course you understand – I don’t love you.”

He: “How could you?!”

She: “Oh, grow up. I’m moving on and you need to, too.”

He: “No. Wait. But, I … I love you.”

She: “You’ll get over it.”

Ashley shook herself mentally. This is not a healthy game to play, she thought. Pulling her inadequately lightweight jacket up snuggly near her neck, she shivered, although she wasn’t sure if it was from the cold or from the melodrama that had played out in her mind. She diverted her gaze away from the couple. It didn’t matter what the words were, it seemed clear to her that they were breaking up and she didn’t want to witness the scene. Neither did she want to hear the words.

Moments later the woman returned to the warmth and the commotion inside the reception hall, but the man lingered. With his back to the brightly lit windows, he kept his head bowed. Ashley glanced between him and the door. She should leave him alone and return to the wedding celebration. Hoping that he was deep in concentration and wouldn’t notice her, Ashley began to step lightly toward the entrance.

After she’d taken a few steps, he still hadn’t noticed her presence. Ashley rushed a couple of steps, hoping to escape without the man ever knowing that she’d been there. She tossed a quick look toward his drooping silhouette. That's when her foot landed on an icy spot below the eave and shot recklessly out from under her. Ashley heard her own gasp and felt herself careening out of control. Feet sliding and arms flailing, she spun as she collided with the wall. As her arm skidded across the surface pulling her jacket sleeve back, the cold, rough bricks bit into the skin from her palm to her elbow. Momentum jerked her other foot out from under her, tipping her backwards. Her head smacked against the wall and pain pulsed at the back of her skull.

By the time she landed inelegantly on the paved patio, the man knelt beside her. Irritation and concern battled in his features, but there was no sign of the pain he had undoubtedly felt when the girlfriend had left him. Neither spoke for a few seconds. Ashley studied the way the light played across the man's features. Muted light from a window tickled his cheek, while the heavy darkness of the midwinter night fought to take him back. The effect was breathtaking. Instinctively, she reached for her bag, groping for her camera. This frame had to be captured.

"Hold still," he spoke quietly. The deep rumble of the command stopped Ashley's movements. "Are you hurt?"

Ashley mutely shook her head slightly, causing the pain in her head to intensify. And then, realizing that as she sat braced against the cold wall, she was cloaked in darkness, she finally responded, "Just my pride."

"You're certain? You didn't break anything?" he asked again. A hint of teasing edged into his deep voice. "You landed pretty hard."

"No. I'm fine," she reasserted.

"I'm Matt," the man declared. He had risen and was bending to grasp her hands in his own, intending to pull Ashley to her feet. Her breath caught and she winced as the tension increased on her left arm. He eased her back down and released her hands. "You *are* hurt."

"It's nothing," she countered. "It has to be nothing."

Before Ashley realized what was happening, Matt had lifted her and set her gently on her feet. "You're shivering," he observed. "Let's get you back inside." He was already steering her toward the entrance as he slipped an arm across her back. Sheltered in the warmth of his nearness, Ashley began to realize how cold she had become lurking in the shadows.

"I'm tough. You don't need to worry about me," she responded.

"Not that tough. You'll catch pneumonia out here," he cautioned as they neared the entrance.

They stepped into the light that shone through the glass doors, and she balked. "We can't go back inside together," she said abruptly.

"Why not?" He seemed genuinely perplexed. "You need a little patching up and besides, you're freezing," he said reasonably.

"People will think …," here voice trailed away. Ashley struggled to remember her reasoning as a shiver racked her body.

A long moment stretched as he regarded her. Finally, he spoke. "What will they think if I leave you out here and return to the party, when you clearly need help?"

"They'll …" she stopped. A wave of dizziness swept over Ashley and she swayed slightly. "You came out here with one girl …" She tried to focus on her own words, but it was becoming difficult. "And. If you come back inside with a different girl …" She swayed again and felt Matt pull her body closer to his. She leaned into him and concluded, “They’ll think you’re easy.”

She felt, more than heard, the reverberation of his low chuckle. “No, sweetheart. They won’t think that,” he asserted. He’d slipped his own jacket off and was wrapping it across her back and over her shoulders.

“What?” Nothing was making sense and her disorientation was escalating. When she reached up with her right hand and gingerly touched the back of her head, she winced. “Ouch!” she exclaimed as her hand came away crimson.

The man deftly turned her and began moving toward the parking lot. “I’m taking you to the doctor,” he announced.

“No.” Ashley stopped abruptly as she made the assertion, but a sick feeling in her stomach stopped her from saying more.

“You have a bleeding head wound. I’m taking you to the doctor,” Matt reiterated, as he pulled her into motion again.

“I can’t leave with you,” she protested weakly. “You could be an axe murderer or something.”

“If I were, you would already be doomed,” he chuckled again. “But you really need to see a doctor.”

Another wave of dizziness hit Ashley, forcing her to lean into the man once more. “My friends will worry,” she whined quietly.

“I’ll let Shelby and Allison know that I have you,” he said as they continued to move with purpose toward a car she presumed was his.

“You know them?” Ashley asked with a note of awe as he deftly opened the passenger side which cast light across her face. Matt regarded her only a moment before helping her inside and pulling the seatbelt across her slender frame to buckle it.

He pulled his cell phone from his pocket as he dashed around to the driver's side. He quickly started the engine and cranked the heater to high. He sent a brief text to his friend, Riley, asking him to let Ashley's friends know that she was safe, before looking again at the woman. "Have you been drinking?" he finally inquired.

"Drinking?" she parroted. Waves of red hair cascaded over her shoulders as she turned slightly to look at him. "No."

"You're certain?"

"Yes." Her brows furrowed over blue eyes. "I mean … no. No drinking." Looking down at her hands, she saw the blood. Her eyes flitted to Matt's in horror as she extended her hand toward the man beside her. "What happened?" she asked in innocent wonder.

It was only about a mile to the hospital, but Matt prayed all the way there.

He quickly arrived at the emergency room of the Miller's Bend hospital with the injured woman and gladly turned Ashley over to the medical staff. After relating the tale of her fall and apparent disorientation and ensuing confusion, he'd been ordered to the waiting room to … well, wait.

Tension tightened the muscles in his neck as Matt leaned forward in the wooden chair with the vintage burnt-orange vinyl cushions. The community of Miller's Bend was lucky to boast a top-quality medical staff, but the facility could definitely use a facelift. Shaking his head at the thought, Matt tried to find a position that would relieve the stress lodged between his shoulder blades and causing a pulsing headache.

It had been a difficult few weeks and he had looked forward to the wedding celebration of two of his friends. Matt had thought the activity and commotion surrounding the wedding would help take his mind off his problems. He was far more concerned with his little sister who left Miller's Bend nearly three weeks ago. She had told him that she was leaving and they'd argued. No, they had fought. Matt tried valiantly to persuade her to stay and finally, arrogantly, had forbidden her from leaving. *Forbid her?* He must have been crazy – he'd known since she was three years old that trying to forbid Chrissi from doing anything would just double or triple her resolve.

Chrissi had left the next day when she should have been in calculus class. He'd received texts from her for the first few days, but then she quit communicating. Their mother had spoken with Chrissi during one phone call, but hadn't learned exactly where she was – just east of South Dakota. That's a lot of territory. How would he find a missing girl whose location is east of South Dakota?

Matt had finally turned to his friend, Mason Alexander, a lawyer who moved to Miller's Bend a few years ago, to assist in the search for his sister. Although Matt's mother seemed to think Chrissi would be home no worse for the wear in a few weeks, Matt was desperate to find her. He'd given Mason all the information he could and now he just needed to wait.

In addition to using the wedding ceremony as a distraction, Matt had also been anxious to attend the reception and dance with Lauren. They'd been dating for a few months, but it seemed more like hanging out with a friend than a serious relationship. He had hoped that the romance and sentimental setting of the wedding would spark something more between them. They'd sat together during the ceremony and the meal and everything seemed normal. They talked with friends and danced together during several numbers after the band began to play.

But as soon as she'd asked him if they could step out on the patio for privacy, his gut clenched. He'd seen the apology in her expression even as he agreed to her request. They retreated from the merriment and when they moved out of the light from the windows, she'd told him goodbye. She didn't belong with him and she didn't belong in Miller's Bend. Lauren would be traveling back to her hometown near Rapid City.

She was leaving. The funny thing was Matt's reaction, or lack of reaction. He should have been hurt or angry, but he wasn't. Lauren was a friend and she was leaving, it wasn't like they'd been deeply involved. He was sad, but not heart-broken. He wasn't even really surprised. After all, people leave. It was nothing new to Matt.

Lauren had returned to the party, leaving Matt alone with his thoughts on the darkened patio. At least he'd thought he was alone, until Ashley crashed into the wall and landed hard on the icy concrete. He'd known who she was because two of his best friends had married two of her best friends, but he doubted she'd known him or anyone else at the party, since she'd barely arrived in time for the ceremony.

Somehow he had become responsible for this woman. It seemed like the right thing to do – getting her to the hospital – but now he was forced to wait and worry about her. As if there was room in his life for more worries.

"I don't need this," he muttered to himself. And then his eyes shifted to the statue of Jesus which graced a wall of the small waiting room. He knew the piece well because he had designed it and created it. Now the likeness of Jesus, holding a small child in one arm and extending the other arm as if beckoning the viewer to join them, reminded him that God takes care of His flock. And members of the flock are supposed to take care of one another.

Matt checked the clock on the wall again – just after midnight. He'd spoken to Riley a few minutes earlier and learned that the bride and groom had left the reception, headed to their honeymoon. He looked up as he heard the sounds of the main entrance door, expecting to see Riley and Shelby dashing in. Instead he noted the arrival of the police chief, Jeff Schuster. The chief spoke briefly with the nurses before turning his attention to Matt.

Rising as the man approached, Matt extended his hand in greeting. "Evening, Mr. Schuster," he offered. The chief, now in his mid-50s had begun to show his age, with a slightly rounded belly and balding head. He seemed friendlier and more fatherly than Matt figured a police chief should, but maybe that was just because he knew the other man so well.

"Evening, Matt," the older man replied as they shook hands. "Let's have a little talk."

"Yes, sir." Matt had first met Jeff Schuster more than a decade earlier, when his mom moved Matt and his sister to this little town in the plains of South Dakota. He'd been in eighth grade, which is about the worst point in a boy's life to uproot him and move him into a new school in a state far, far away from everything he knows.

Matt had tried to fit in, but it had been hard. He didn't do well in class and wasn't athletic enough to make the sports teams. A growth spurt had pushed him to an unreasonable height just months after his arrival in Miller's Bend. He'd felt like a freak and a few of the kids amplified the feeling by the way they treated him.

His life had been miserable, until the day when he'd stumbled upon Riley Wheeler and Tyler Schuster making a poor attempt at vandalizing the side wall of a garage. Matt burst into laughter when he saw the pitiful graffiti the pair had painted on that wall. They'd taken him down and roughed him up, but when he regained his feet, he continued to laugh.

"I suppose you think you can do better?" one of them challenged. Matt picked up his backpack without replying and began walking away when a can of spray paint whizzed past his head and landed in his pathway. He'd turned, half expecting to be tackled again, but Riley's laughing eyes told him he was in the clear.

Matt picked up the spray can and, with it and several other colors, proceeded to work on the garage-art project. Absorbed in the details of painting, he worked without realizing where he was, whether the other two boys had stayed or gone, or how late was getting. He painted until he was out of paint and when he turned, he'd been greeted by not only Riley and Tyler, but also an ancient-looking woman, his own mother, and the fathers of the other boys – Lawrence Wheeler and Jeff Schuster. Tyler's father had been wearing a police uniform.

The ancient woman turned out to be Mrs. Holmes who owned the garage. She said she rather liked the artwork, but thought the boys should be punished by painting the exterior of her house – white. During the summer of painting, Tyler, Riley and Matt became bonded as brothers. Mrs. Holmes became a surrogate grandmother to the trio. She also had taken it upon herself to push a good amount of religious exposure on the young men. If they protested, she'd threaten to call their parents, which was in truth a veiled threat to turn them over to the law. The townspeople and teachers dubbed the trio "the posse" and the moniker stuck.

The police chief cleared his throat meaningfully, bringing Matt's thoughts back to the present. He gestured toward a row of chairs, indicating that Matt should sit. "This is official," Jeff said with authority as he reached for his notebook. “The hospital staff called it in as a possible abuse.”

“Of course they did,” Matt acknowledged with a slight nod. His head was pounding as he lowered himself back into the chair from which he had risen.

“How long have you known the victim?” Jeff queried.

A deep sigh escaped as Matt held the chief’s gaze. “She’s not a victim. She fell,” Matt replied quietly with a slight shake of his head. “I seated her at the beginning of Andrew and Allison Wheeler’s wedding …” He paused and glanced toward the clock again before continuing, “About seven hours ago. I first spoke to her outside of the reception hall about an hour ago.”

“Full name?”

“Her’s?” Matt asked. He concentrated for a moment before replying, “She didn’t say. She’s one of Shelby Wheeler’s best friends. Shelby’s and Allison’s. First name is Ashley.”

The hospital doors whooshed open and Shelby surged frantically into the lobby area. Glancing quickly around the spacious area, she spotted Matt and Jeff seated in the waiting area and bolted toward them. Riley, who had followed closely behind his wife, turned to speak to the nurses before catching up.

“What happened?!” Shelby asked with a note of desperation. “Is Ashley alright?” Her gaze darted between Matt and the police chief.

“Evening, Shelby,” the chief drawled. “Care to have a seat?” It was really a command, not an invitation, but the slight woman ignored his authority.

“Is Ashley alright?” she demanded a second time.

“We don’t know yet. She’s still being examined,” Jeff said patiently. Then glancing to Riley, he said, “Maybe we could all have a seat." Riley nodded and gently guided Shelby into the chair next to Matt before taking a seat himself.

With pen poised over the notebook, the chief directed his statement to Matt. "Tell me what happened."

Matt calmly recounted the events until Shelby noted Dr. Stapp who quickly approached the group. She rose to meet him. "How's Ashley?"

"Does the young lady have any family we can call?" he asked without addressing the query. "We need to get her medical history. Things aren't making sense."

"Her immediate family lives near the Twin Cities," Shelby replied. "The number's got to be in her phone." Then turning to Matt, she asked, "Where's her bag? It would be in there."

"We've got it, Shelby. Tried the emergency number but there's no answer," the young doctor replied. "Without her medical history, it's kind of a guessing game."

"I thought the hospital was part of a national system and the database was accessible throughout the country, no matter where a person gets treated?" the chief interjected.

"It is. But we can't find Miss Nightingale in the system," he replied.

"Miss Nightingale?" Shelby echoed. "Who is that?"

"Ashley Nightingale," Dr. Stapp replied as he looked to the woman. "That's the name she gave us."

Confusion clouded her expression before Shelby blurted, "Her name is Ashley Nelson." She delivered the information stressing and clearly enunciating the last name. Dread clutched at Shelby as things fell into place. "Oh, no," she gasped, and then raising her gaze to meet the doctor's she asked, "Does she have a concussion again?"

"Again?"

Shelby was aware that Riley was supporting her, although she didn't know just when he had moved to her side and wrapped her in his embrace. She focused on the doctor in front of her. "Ashley Nelson has been diagnosed with concussions at least four times that I know of. Maybe more. She was hospitalized after a brutal attack in Brookings four years ago. I think that was the first concussion. The others happened when she was on assignment in various locations around the world. I don't know if you can find all her medical records or not. She's been so many places," Shelby explained.

CHAPTER TWO

Everything was annoying to him, and Matt resented that he possessed the self-awareness to realize that it was his own sour mood which caused the irritation. Nothing had gone bad in a big way … it was just more of the same. He hadn't accomplished anything in his studio, he hadn't heard any news about his sister, and his mom was the same as most days. Even the juke box music in the bar portion of the restaurant was irritating. Rising, he grabbed his set of darts from the table as he moved toward the throwing line. He and his friends Riley, Andrew and Tyler, played together in a league dart team during the winter months. With Andrew being away on his honeymoon, they had called on Mason Alexander to step in as a substitute on the team.

Matt shook off the worries that had been plaguing him and tried to focus on launching the dart into the bull's-eye on the board before him. Drawing a deep breath, he let the dart fly, hitting its mark. His second dart also nestled into the red center of the board. As he was poised to release his final dart of the turn, one of the other team's players called out, "Any word about your sister?"

Irritation pulsed through Matt's mind as his dart went wide – no points for that one. He moved forward and retrieved his darts so a player from the other team could begin his turn before Matt responded. The delay also gave him a moment to decide how to answer. "I'm sure we'll hear any day now," he answered with a glance toward his teammates. They were best of friends, and each of them shared his despair over not being able to help Chrissi. Help her? They hadn't even been able to find her! Mason's gaze dropped as Matt returned to the table.

"We'll find her," Riley assured him as he gave Matt a quick pat on the shoulder.

Tyler added, "You bet we will. And I'll be your wingman to help you bring her back." He clapped a hand on Matt's shoulder as he passed on his way to the line to take his turn in the dart game.

Concern shadowed Mason's expression, but he didn't add to the pep talk. He'd been looking into Chrissi's disappearance and had not been able to give Matt any good news – actually, he'd had nothing but bad news. He took a drink of his cola and set it down, wishing he had a good cold beer instead, as he would have in his college years. The only consolation to having given up alcoholic drinks, was that he had friends who also abstained from drinking. Theirs was a religious choice, while his had been career insurance. Despite the fact that he'd settled in the tiny little community of Miller's Bend to practice law, he had aspirations of running for political offices. DUI charges and other embarrassing incidents had been known to resurface years later for candidates, and he didn't want to generate any mistakes that would sideline his career. To that end … no booze.

"How's your mom holding up?" Riley asked when Matt had completed his next turn. "Is she feeling alright?"

With a slight shrug, Matt answered with a noncommittal, "Mostly."

Riley's attitude was subdued as he leaned toward his friend. "You know any one of us will help out anytime you need us …"

He let his voice trail away because Matt was already shaking his head in denial of the offer. "She's my responsibility," he answered solemnly. "I won't pass her off to someone else. Not even you."

"You are a stubborn cuss. You know that?" It was Tyler who cut in now. "You don't have to take all the responsibility for everyone in your family. Maybe if you'd let Chrissi help, she wouldn't have taken off."

Matt's gazed jerked toward Tyler and his eyes narrowed. "You're blaming me for her leaving? You know I've been taking care of Chrissi since her dad left us. You know that I've sacrificed to do what's best for her and for Mom."

Tyler leaned across the table in response to Matt's reaction. "Yeah, I know," he spoke loudly. Swinging his arm in an encompassing gesture he added in a rising voice, "We all know. You wear it like a badge of honor. You take care of everything for everybody in your life."

The dart board flashed as the opposing team took the win in that game. Since Mason and Riley would be playing in the next matchup, neither Tyler nor Matt would need to focus on the game for a while. "That's right," Matt declared. "I do take care of Mom and Chrissi – there hasn't been anyone else available for the job for more than 15 years," he hissed. "Where's the crime in that?"

Mason wore a stern expression as he intervened. "Are you guys sure you want to do this here?" he asked as he raised his focus to the patrons at the next table. "You're drawing an audience."

"I want to clear this up," Matt said in a low voice. Leveling an icy glare at his friend, he stated, "I didn't drive Chrissi away."

Tyler forced himself to relax back into his chair to try to calm the atmosphere. He didn't want to fight with his friend; he just wanted to make his point. "Yah, Buddy. I know you wouldn't intentionally push her away," he said quietly. "What I mean is that she's a lot like you are … she's a caregiver … and with you busy taking responsibility for her and your mom, there's nobody for Chrissi to fuss over and dote on."

"She's just a kid and she needs to be taking care of her grades," Matt countered. "She's got SATs coming up and college applications to fill out. I can handle everything else."

"Do you think she's making a lot of progress there?" Tyler asked. And then with blatant sarcasm he added quietly, "Since she's disappeared, I'll bet those are real high priorities for her."

"Knock it off, Ty," Riley advised from beside the table. "I don't want to have to bail you two out of jail for brawling." Riley shifted his focus to Matt and he added, "We all know you've got it handled. It's just …" He paused as he searched for the words. "It's just that, well, sometimes it's alright to accept some help. Let your friends back you up."

Matt glared, first at Tyler as he declared, "I didn't drive her off." And, since his friends were being unreasonable, he figured he could be too, so he glared at Riley. "And I don't need anybody's help."

The following morning Matt sat despondently in Mason's law office as he listened to Mason's words. Matt had suffered through a lousy day followed by a lousy night. Completely stressed out, he had snapped at his friends and stormed out of the bar. He hadn't slept well as he struggled with worries about his mom and sister, and money. On top of everything else, he felt guilty about his response to Tyler's jibes, and Riley's attempts to smooth things over.

"Matt?" Mason's voice broke into his thoughts. "Are you even listening?"

"Why didn't you tell me this last night?" he asked as he bolted to his feet in frustration and paced in front of the sleek desk.

Mason cocked a brow before replying, "In the bar? You wanted me to discuss this while you were throwing darts?"

"No," he growled. A moment passed as Mason waited for the information to sink in. "Colorado? That doesn't make sense; she told us she was east of here. You're sure she's in Boulder?"

Mason nodded.

"How did she disappear once she got there?" Matt inquired.

Mason had already explained that he'd obtained her cell phone records and her debit card transactions. He surmised that his friend had meant, how had he lost her trail? "She ditched the cell phone and quit using the debit card," Mason offered in explanation. "I'd guess she knew you'd be looking for her and intentionally terminated her trail."

Matt nodded as he considered the possible courses of action. "I should go to Boulder …," he began.

"And what? You plan to just walk the streets until you find her?" Mason asked. Without waiting for a reply, he continued, "She's probably not there anyway."

Matt swiveled to face the man he was paying to find his sister. "What do you mean? You just said you followed her trail to Boulder!"

"She's a smart woman, Matt," Mason explained as he flipped open his briefcase. "Don't you think she knew you'd be after her?"

"Girl. She's a girl, a kid, and we have to find her before something happens," Matt enunciated slowly, carefully keeping his irritation in check. "I have to go look for her!"

Mason circled the desk and stopped Matt's pacing. They both knew Matt couldn't go after her – he had a responsibility to his mother. "Your mom needs you. Let your friends help you out. And please, let me get the police chief in on this. We can use his resources in the search."

"Mom doesn't want to involve the law. She's confident that Chrissi is just expressing her independence and will be home soon," Matt spoke the words slowly as if he didn't like the sound of them coming off his tongue. "She says I'm making a mountain out of a mole hill and I should pray for patience and have some faith."

Mason snorted before replying, "Maybe she's right. But if it was my sister, I wouldn't let up until I located her." He strode toward the door with Matt, "Think about it – why would she go to Boulder? Is there someone she would turn to there? If there is, I'd recommend making some calls before you run after her. She could be long gone by the time you arrive – probably has already moved on."

"There's a possibility that she'd contact …," Matt was thinking aloud and glanced back to Mason. "Never mind. I'll check with a couple of people and get back to you."

Nearly one-year-old twins, Jacob and Isabelle, played quietly as they sat on a blanket spread over a section of living room floor in Ashley's new, temporary apartment in the basement of Mrs. Holmes' home. Ashley had spent a couple of nights in the hospital, and one night on the couch at Riley and Shelby's home before arrangements had been made to get Ashley into her own place. Shelby and her children had arrived that afternoon with some gifts to make the place homier for Ashley while she rested and waited for her memory to return. "I'm really sorry that you can't stay with us," Shelby said sweetly. "We're just lucky Mrs. Holmes doesn't have any renters right now." The women had finished their decorating and were enjoying cookies and tea as they relaxed. "So, how's it going?" Shelby queried gently. "Memories coming back yet?"

With a shake of her head, Ashley replied, "Nothing." Her frustration had grown in the days since she'd been released from the hospital. Her memory of long-ago events and basic knowledge of herself were strong. She'd discovered that with a great deal of effort and concentration she could take in and recall new information, but sometimes it could just as easily slip away from her. It seemed she had to write notes about everything and repeat details to herself before her mind would latch onto them and keep the information available for recall. "I'm afraid I'll have to keep my notebook with me every minute. It's so hard to make anything stick," she said as she bumped her head with the heel of her hand.

That development – being unable to remember things – was irritating enough, however, her mind had also blocked out a specific time period. The latest concussion had caused memory loss, not only of the night of Allison and Andrew's wedding, but most of the preceding weeks. That month or so included a great deal of research into a news story – a big story – that Ashley couldn't recall. She also couldn't recall where she had safely stashed her research and evidence that she had amassed. At least that's what she had thought – until she had called her employer to explain her accident, hospitalization and need for medical leave.

"And then there's the mystery of my job," she added as though it were of little consequence.

"What about your job?" Shelby asked with concern rising in her voice. "They aren't giving you a hard time about the medical leave are they?"

"Not technically," Ashley answered. She paced over to the babies and moved some toys which had escaped from the blanket back into easy reach before turning to meet her friend's gaze. Ashley sighed as she remembered the conversation with her boss, Mr. Luctin.

"I called Mr. Luctin and he listened quietly as I explained that I'd fallen and suffered from another concussion. I told him the doctor had diagnosed me with mild amnesia," Ashley recited distractedly. She moved back to the couch to sit near her friend. "I told him I was sorry, but I won't be able to return to work until my memories resurface. I said that could be any day," she had rushed to explain. "I just needed time off until I can remember what I was working on and where I stashed the research," she had concluded.

"That all seems reasonable," Shelby observed. "What happened?"

Ashley looked away as she recalled the confusion she'd felt when Mr. Luctin had responded gently, "I'd imagine that it's hard for you, with the amnesia, and being stuck in that small town, but Ashley …" he'd paused and cleared his throat. "Don't you remember? You resigned." There had been a long moment while neither spoke. And then her former boss had added quietly, "I wish you all the best, but you quit your job here. You left us."

Meeting her friend's inquiring gaze, Ashley straightened her spine and inhaled. "Apparently, I had resigned before leaving for Miller's Bend."

A squeal of delight shot from Shelby as she grabbed Ashley in a quick hug. "That's fantastic!" she exclaimed. "What are you planning to do?"

Ashley squirmed away from the hug. "It's not fantastic! I loved that job. What could I have been thinking?!"

"What do you mean?"

"I don't remember quitting – or even considering quitting. How could I have done something so reckless?"

Even now, after dwelling on the conversation for hours, Ashley couldn't quite believe that she would have done such a thing. She had pressed Mr. Luctin for information – had something happened? Had she been upset? What was her reason for quitting the job that she loved? He remained adamant that he hadn't known her thinking or her plans for the future. "You wouldn't tell me why you were leaving or where you were going," he had said. "But I'm sure that you had a plan," he'd added.

Ashley was certain that she had been working on a story. She had been researching and amassed a stockpile of information that she wasn't ready to share with anyone. A secret – she had a secret. That idea didn't mesh with what Mr. Luctin said. He insisted that she had completed her work and turned in everything. He surmised that if she had more information squirreled away, that it was in regard to a personal project … or her next job.

"I called my mom to see if I'd told her my plans," Ashley related. "She was way too happy to hear the news, but she didn't know anything about it." Again, Ashley searched her friend's expression. "Did I tell you what was going on? Did I tell you that I quit my job; did I have something else lined up?"

"I'm pretty sure I'd remember if you had told me," Shelby replied quickly. She jumped up and hugged her friend again before adding, "I'm just so excited for you! You can finally have a safe normal job –"

"Don't you see? I loved that job. It was my purpose, my reason for being," Ashley confided with tears brimming in her eyes. "Without it, what will I do? Who will I be?"

"Oh, no. No you don't, Ashley Nelson," Shelby came to her side as she spoke. "You know who you are and we both know it was time for a change from that job, before you were seriously hurt or maybe even killed. God had revealed another path to you – one that you were apparently ready to travel until you lost your memory. You have to pray for the patience and the faith that He will lead you back to His intended path for you."

Ashley wiped her eyes and sniffled, before giving Shelby a shaky smile. "I will try to be patient," she said quietly. "It's just hard. It's like I don't know my own mind … and I don't have anything to do. I'm used to being busy," she sighed. "I'm not patient and, well, it's just hard."

An idea had been niggling Shelby and she had a feeling that the time was right to give voice to it. "Hey, Ashley? You remember how to write a news story don't you?"

"Well, yes. As a matter of fact, I believe I could manage that," Ashley replied. Then with suspicion, she added a slow, "Why do you ask?"

CHAPTER THREE

Miller's Bend, South Dakota. Ashley stood on the front step of her apartment and looked down the street in the quiet town. She struggled to hold on to the reason she was here. It wasn't an exotic place, there was no riot, no government overthrow, no political dignitary in town, no news whatsoever in the burg. Miller's Bend was no more than a wide spot in the road where some ancient traders decided to meet by the river's edge.

According to the kind, ghost of a woman, Mrs. Holmes, who owned the majestic Victorian style home that included Ashley's apartment, settlers had begun frequenting the trading area and permanent structures had been built in the early 1800s. Homes had been constructed as the area was homesteaded and some decades later, the industrious Miller Family took the initiative to get the townspeople to incorporate and the name Miller's Bend was chosen to honor the family.

While she was hospitalized, Ashley's parents had come to her. They had insisted on taking her home with them, but Ashley staunchly refused. "I've been taking care of myself for a long time," she explained. "I will manage. Besides, I'm sure my memory will be fine tomorrow." Several "tomorrows" had come, but her memory had not returned. Her parents stayed in Miller's Bend only a few days before returning home and leaving Ashley in Shelby's care. They also took care of returning the car Ashley had rented at the airport when she arrived for Allison and Andrew's wedding.

Now, with her camera cradled on her bandaged wrist, Ashley pulled a borrowed hunter-orange stocking cap further onto her head, took a deep, chilling breath and began her trek toward the business district of the small town. She wasn't a stranger to faith and since her hospitalization, she'd been praying that she would regain her memory. She prayed that her new job would reveal itself, somehow. She prayed that it was all a mistake or a joke or … whatever would explain away the current circumstances and let her get back to her life. But Shelby's words kept replaying in her mind: *You have to pray for the patience and the faith that He will lead you back to His intended path for you.* "But I don't want patience," she mumbled under her breath as she marched toward her goal.

Walking quickly toward the town's Main Street, Ashley listened to the crunch of the snow beneath her feet and wondered why she was even bothering with the interview that Shelby had arranged with the owner of the Chronicle. It was a weekly newspaper in a small rural community in South Dakota – it didn't represent any of the things Ashley wanted for herself. For heaven's sake, she had no aspirations to stay in a small town, and the moment her memory returned, she planned to get a ride to the nearest airport and board a plane for the next world assignment. One small problem: she had resigned from that job.

Ashley had spent hours on the phone trying to find out if she had told anyone her plans. No one knew anything that could help her unravel the mystery she'd created for herself. Dismayed at her own lack of foresight, Ashley had resigned herself to Shelby's suggestion that she check with Catherine, owner of the Chronicle, Miller's Bend's community newspaper, to see if she could do some freelance writing until she got her bearings again.

Unsettling. The whole situation was unsettling. As she waited for a "walk" signal at one of the few stoplights in town, she pulled the reporter's notebook from the pocket of her leather jacket. In an act of reassurance, she glanced at the page where she had recorded her own basic information – just in case the amnesia worsened. She doubted that she could ever forget who she was at her core, but she was more than a little scared. She read the lines of her own handwriting: Ashley Nelson, 26, from Rogers, MN. Graduate of SDSU department of journalism, researcher for a major network news organization. Parents: Tammie and Chuck Nelson. Brothers: Tom and Scott. Best friends: Allison and Shelby.

On the second page of the notebook, she had written other information. Some she had known and some she'd been told: Shelby married Riley Wheeler nearly two years ago and they had twins, Jacob and Isabelle. Allison married Andrew Wheeler the night of Ashley's fall, and they were still traveling on their honeymoon. Their newly formed family included Allison's daughter, Hope, and Andrew's daughter, Rori. Ashley had arrived in the small town just in time to attend the wedding. She had slipped, fallen and hit her head during the reception. Too many concussions = memory loss. Temporary?

It was an unseasonably warm day for winter on the plains, but despite the sun's rays, Ashley began to feel the sting of the wind by the time she arrived at the entrance to the office of the Chronicle. Stepping inside she shivered slightly and closed the door tightly behind her. "Hello?" she called when she realized there was no one in the front office. Settling her camera on the counter, Ashley gazed slowly around the room.

Dusty shelves displayed a smattering of trophies with engraved plaques: Little League Baseball sponsor, Cougar Kits Football, 4-H, Chamber Business of the Month, Historical Society Donor, and many others. The small-town newspaper was obviously a supporter of many organizations in the community. Ashley knew that Shelby enjoyed the time that she had spent as a reporter for the Chronicle before the birth of her babies led her to be a stay-at-home mom. Shelby appreciated the tightly-knit town and had been truly interested in the events and people she wrote about. But that was the life for Shelby – Ashley loved the fast-paced career she thrived on in the city – at least until she quit, she thought with a shake of her head.

Photos of President Eisenhower and a man Ashley didn't recognize dominated two of the walls, while smaller framed prints showed groups of people in the Oval Office with Former Presidents Clinton and Carter. Other photos showed an elderly couple posing with unnamed politicians. Ashley assumed these were state-level dignitaries.

Numerous plaques, each one shaped like the state of South Dakota, graced the final wall. Each of them was an award earned in the Better Newspaper Contest in various categories including newswriting, photography, advertising and sports reporting. She was scanning the inscriptions on them when she heard approaching footsteps – more of a shuffling than a stepping, but someone was approaching from another part of the building. Ashley turned and found herself facing the elderly woman who was pictured in the photos with the politicians. This was Catherine.

Stepping close to the counter and extending her hand, Ashley introduced herself. The rotund woman responded with a "come here" wave presented from about belly-button height. "Come on around the end of the counter and let's go sit in the private office a few minutes," Catherine directed. "It's more comfortable." As the older woman began to move toward the back of the building she said something that sounded like, "I didn't realize you would be here so soon."

"I'm sorry," Ashley offered as she complied with the instructions and began to follow. "I was sure I had the time correct. I can come back later if that would be better."

The woman was shuffling away, toddling a bit as she moved toward the farthest room in the building. She didn't turn toward Ashley, but said, "No, no. You've got the right time; I just didn't expect you until next week."

Catherine's words confused Ashley, and she stopped following. *Next week?* "Come on then," Catherine encouraged, "I want you to meet everyone. Pour yourself a cup of coffee and come to the back room."

Ashley glanced at the coffee pot which was chugging and bubbling away. She was carrying her bag with samples of her writing and photos as well as her camera, and of course she had the awkward bandages on her left wrist. Adding coffee to the mix seemed like a recipe for disaster. "Thank you. I think I'll pass on the coffee for now," she said.

The people in the room stopped talking when the two paraded through the doorway. "Pull up a chair," Catherine directed as she dropped into an old vinyl covered chair with wooden arms. Then she looked at Ashley who stood frozen in the doorway. "I want you to sit here," the older woman said as she pointed to a man who was seated near her. "So I can have a good look at you." Turning toward the man, she added, "You can get another chair."

His insulted expression didn't hide the disdain as well as his voice did when he responded, "Of course, Catherine. Anything to make it easier for you." He didn't look Ashley's direction as he rose and moved gracefully to another chair.

"Everybody … This is Shelby's friend, Ashley," Catherine said as she picked up her Styrofoam cup and sipped. "Tell us about yourself." Pale blue eyes looked Ashley's way as she settled into the indicated chair. Cradling her camera in her lap, Ashley slid her bag under the chair. She glanced from face to face and wondered what to say.

Squirming like a kid in the principal's office, she finally said, "I thought this was supposed to be an interview?" She felt the heat rising in her cheeks and knew that her discomfort showed. "I'm sorry. I must have been mistaken." She began to rise, but Catherine stopped her.

"I don't need to interview you," Catherine said. "Of course the job is yours. We just want to get to know you."

Resettling, Ashley was amazed. "No interview?" Ashley had been working in an industry with intense competition for job openings and Catherine's easy-going manner unnerved her a bit. "What do you mean? Don't you want to see the samples of my work?"

Shaking her head moderately, Catherine replied, "Heavens, no." She slurped another sip of coffee before turning to the unhappy man who had been forced to give up his seat, "Could you get me a refill?" Without a word, he rose to retrieve the coffee carafe.

Redirecting to Ashley, Catherine again commanded, "Tell us about yourself. We haven't had a reporter with world-wide experience before. I worked in DC when I was younger, but I didn't do any international work."

Ashley had never been in a situation like this before and her mind scrambled for the right answer. "Well … I'm Ashley Nelson. I've been working for a major news network, but before I got picked up there, I had worked in smaller markets. I do the research and the writing, but not the on-air work."

"What countries have you traveled to?" asked a kind-looking woman seated at another desk. "I think it would be exciting to travel." Ashley estimated the woman to be about the age of her own parents. The woman seemed genuinely interested in getting to know her.

"Now, Bobbie," Catherine said, "Don't interrupt the girl." She sipped at her coffee again before turning to Ashley. "You graduated from SDSU?"

"Yes, that's right," she replied with a note of bewilderment.

"Are you Catholic? I haven't seen you at Mass," Catherine forged ahead.

"No. I'm not."

"Well? What are you?"

"I don't think you can ask me that," Ashley countered.

A short snort preceded Catherine's, reply, "Of course I can. I just did. You're not one of those atheists, are you?"

"I'm Methodist, but …"

"Good! Everyone who works here is either Catholic or Methodist," Catherine declared. "You'll fit right in." She paused to sip at her coffee again.

The man finally spoke. "I think you're forgetting something, Catherine." He spoke with a passive voice, but Ashley sensed that the man was seething within.

"Oh, that's right. Neal here is …" Catherine paused as her brows drew down in concentration. "What is it? Episcopalian?"

"Presbyterian."

"Are you sure?"

"Of course, I'm sure, Catherine."

Catherine peered at the man for a moment before looking again to Ashley. "And you're a Democrat, I'm sure."

Remembering the photos displayed in the front office, Ashley nodded mutely. It really didn't matter which party her affiliation was – she surely wasn't going to start another round of controversy.

"Good." Catherine seemed to realize that introductions hadn't been completed. She proceeded to introduce her husband and business partner of 52 years, Charlie; the reporter, Neal; the bookkeeper and front desk helper, Bobbie, and a young graphic artist, Tim.

"Do you want to start today or tomorrow?" Catherine asked as the others disbanded to return to their work.

"I think tomorrow would be fine," Ashley said, still somewhat dazed by the events. She buttoned her coat, slipped her hands into mittens and collected her bag and camera and looked at Catherine again. She found herself wondering if it would be a mistake to take the job – even on a temporary basis.

Ashley trailed the others toward the front of the building and when they reached the lobby, Catherine spoke abruptly. "Alright. I'll see you at nine," she commanded. Then with a softer tone, she added, "Tell Shelby we miss her."

Ashley assured the older woman that she would relay the message to Shelby, said her goodbyes and stepped out into the sunshine and the wind and began walking toward Mrs. Holmes' place. Maybe it would be fun – like an adventure – to be working at the Chronicle for a brief time, Ashley told herself. The doctor had strongly recommended that Ashley not return to work until she had her wits about her again. He'd ordered her to relax until she felt better. She did feel better. She felt restless. And since that disturbing phone conversation with Mr. Luctin, she'd been confused and worried. By all accounts, Ashley wasn't the type who would walk away from responsibility for no reason. And she surely wouldn't quit one job without another lined up and waiting. So … where was she supposed to be working? Ashley didn't have a clue.

Deep in concentration, she was surprised when a man strode up beside her. "Good morning, Ashley," he addressed her with familiarity. She paused and looked up into his face. Cheerful, crystal blue eyes assessed her and a smile blossomed as he watched her. "You don't remember me, do you?" he asked with a hint of playfulness.

"No, I'm sorry. I don't," she replied. "You're familiar, but I can't quite …" She stopped as she concentrated on a wavering ghost of an image in her mind. The almost-memory was gone, dancing away around a corner in her mind. "Sorry. No," she said as she lowered her eyes.

"Hey, it's okay. I'm Matt. Matt Vander Meer," he said as they began walking again. "I was there on the patio when you fell."

"Oh?" She tried again to pull up a memory of Allison and Andrew's wedding, but failed. A few moments passed and he continued to walk with her. "Were you the one who took care of me? Who took me to the hospital?"

"That would be me," he confirmed with a nod. "Aiding damsels in distress is my sideline." He bowed deeply for her benefit.

She laughed. "Are there many of them here in Miller's Bend? Damsels in distress, I mean."

He leaned close and with a conspiratorial whisper, suggested, "More than you might guess." The remark was accentuated with a wink. And the combination had Ashley laughing again.

"You mean there's more to this town than meets the eye?" she challenged. "There are secrets?"

"I'll never tell," he replied.

"I have ways of making you talk," she joked in a sinister voice. "You will be putty in my hands!"

Matt glanced away. As he looked around, he asked, "Where's your car? I'll walk you to it."

"I don't have one," she offered. "I walked uptown."

"Brrr! Aren't you frozen?" he asked with exaggerated shivering of his own.

"Naw. You know I'm tough," she said with a laugh. Immediately, the two stopped and faced each other.

Matt's face lit with hope. "You remember? That was part of what you said the night you fell! You told me you weren't cold because you are tough."

Ashley concentrated on trying to pull the memory to the forefront of her consciousness. She stood next to the man who had befriended her when she fell, trying desperately to remember what had happened. She looked up into his expectant gaze, and with moisture in her eyes, she replied, "No. I don't remember."

Ashley had met with more frustration in the past week than she'd encountered in some time. Trying to force herself to remember the missing time block seemed to force it further from her mental reach. She'd tried focusing, concentrating, meditating, relaxing, and various herbal drinks. Nothing helped.

"You almost did," he countered as he took her by the elbow and steered her into a small coffee shop. Ashley noted the sign on the door read "The Daily Grind". "Let's warm up and we can talk some more," he suggested. "That is, if you have time?" Ashley didn't really believe talking with Matt would help. But then again, she reasoned, it wouldn't likely hurt either.

After ordering a hot chocolate and a latte, they settled into a booth facing each other. "So …" Ashley paused to slip her coat off. "You're Matt, Rescuer of Damsels."

"Yes, but you can just call me Matt when we are in public, if you don't mind," he countered with a broad smile. "I try to keep a low profile." The store owner, Karla, appeared with their drinks, depositing them deftly and returning to the kitchen area.

"I'll bet that's a challenge – keeping a low profile, I mean," Ashley countered. "You do kind of stick out in the crowd."

"Have you seen me in a crowd?"

Ashley searched her blank memory for an image of the man. "I must have seen you at the wedding, but I don't remember. You surely would have stood out. You're so tall and …," she spoke quietly. She'd been about to add "handsome" to her statement, but realizing that would be inappropriate, she let her voice trail away. Looking down at her hands, she felt her cheeks burning, "I just wish I could remember."

"Your memory will come back when you are ready to deal with your real life again," he predicted gently.

"You sound as though you think I lost my memory on purpose," she countered before sipping the white chocolate caramel latte. "It's really inconvenient and it messed up my work. And my life." A scowl crossed her features as she recalled the situation.

"No, I don't mean to imply that," he said as he watched Ashley. The sun streaming through the large display window played across her cheek. Subconsciously, Matt studied the lines and planes of her face and slender neck, wishing he could begin to sculpt her likeness. He continued to scrutinize Ashley until he was overcome with the sense that he had somehow intruded. Mentally redirecting his thoughts, he tried to recall where they had left the conversation hanging.

"Why are you staring at me?"

"I … uh …," he glanced away as he said quietly, "Never mind. It doesn't matter."

"Well it does matter to me," she said. "That was kind of … weird – the way you were looking at me." She waited, noting that Matt seemed uncomfortable.

She took another drink as she waited.

Finally, with downcast eyes, he spoke quietly, "I was just lost in thought. That's all." When he raised his focus to meet Ashley's gaze, he prompted, "So, what are you doing uptown?"

Accepting the evasive explanation, she decided to take the bait and change topics. "I met the staff of the Chronicle. I start work tomorrow," she said wistfully. "It seems that I rashly quit my previous job before coming to Miller's Bend for the wedding, although I don't remember a thing about it," she explained, touching her temple with a forefinger. "Catherine has some freelance work for me."

Matt laughed heartily as Ashley related the story of the interview that wasn't. "I can't believe she'd hire me without even looking at the samples of my photos and my writing. I've been working in research recently and haven't published anything since college, but I'm confident the samples provide a good representation of my talents," Ashley concluded.

Ashley was surprised when Matt tapped her bag, which she had laid on the table. "I'd love to see your work," he suggested. She hesitated before responding and in that moment, Matt withdrew. Letting his gaze flicker to something outside the window, he simultaneously pulled his hand back to grasp his coffee cup and shifted slightly downward in his seat.

Following his line of vision, Ashley saw an old man getting out of a nearly ancient, rust-gutted pickup in front of the post office and, a short distance away, a couple strolling hand-in-hand toward a parked SUV. The pair laughed and leaned toward each other as they walked. Glancing again toward the man across the table, she whispered, "I'm sorry, Matt."

"Why?" he countered as he pulled his attention back to Ashley. "Why would you be sorry?" he repeated as he watched her intently. He shifted forward again, almost like a parent coaching a small child, wanting to provide the answer, but knowing it is better for the child to come up with it on their own. He waited.

Slowly lowering her gaze, she shook her head. "I don't know why. I just know that you have my sympathy," she finally answered. "You lost something or someone. It was important though," she reflected. "You're sad, and hurting. Do you want to tell me about it?"

Matt tipped his head slightly as though trying to decipher a hidden message before replying. "Not today. But thank you," he said in a deeply vibrating tone that was barely audible from across the table. "I'm not ready to discuss it." They sat in silence while each considered their own thoughts. Their drinks were gone, but neither seemed in a particular hurry to leave the booth in the little coffee shop in the quiet town on the plains.

Eventually, Karla appeared and asked if they needed anything before she collected their cups and disappeared. "I guess, I'd better get back to Mrs. Holmes' before she starts to worry about me," Ashley said quietly. "I think she's afraid I'll wander off and get lost," she added in a stage whisper.

The light was back in Matt's eyes as he replied, "Lost in Miller's Bend? Now that would be news."

"Maybe so, but she does tend to worry about me more than necessary."

"Well," Matt replied with a wide smile, "In that case, I will personally see you home so you don't cause her any additional distress."

CHAPTER FOUR

Matt was just helping Ashley from his car when Mrs. Holmes appeared in the doorway of her home. "Oh, good! You're back," Mrs. Holmes called, almost as though she'd been waiting and watching for Ashley's return.

The two returned the greeting before Ashley whispered, "See what I mean? She worries way too much about me."

"It's nice to have someone who is concerned about you," Matt replied quietly. "She pretty much adopts all of her renters. It's good for both her and them." Ashley had reached back into the car to retrieve her bag and her camera. As she turned and straightened, a wave of dizziness overtook her. She reflexively grabbed for something sturdy to steady herself.

When her head cleared, she realized that although she'd grasped the car door, it was Matt's strong hands that held her, gently keeping her righted. She peered up into the concerned face of the man who had not yet loosened his grip. No words came to her as he regarded her solemnly. Finally, he asked, "Does that happen often?"

"Well," she quipped, "You did say rescuing damsels is your sideline."

A quick smile flirted with his features before he quickly cloaked it. “I meant the dizziness,” he clarified. “Does it happen often? And is it related to the concussion?”

With a slight nod and a shrug she answered, “The doctor said it could happen from time to time until I recover.” Pulling her toward himself, Matt closed the car door. And then with his hand to the small of her back, he guided her to the entrance where Mrs. Holmes had disappeared. When Ashley tried to turn to the door of her own apartment which was in the basement of the home, Matt explained gently, “She’ll be expecting us to join her for a few minutes.”

Matt convinced Mrs. Holmes that he and Ashley had recently snacked, when she would have insisted on serving treats. “In that case, you will just have to come back another time and I’ll treat you then,” the grandmotherly woman declared as the trio had settled in the sitting room.

After a few minutes of small talk, she turned her attention to Ashley “What did you think of Catherine and everyone at the Chronicle?” Ashley’s glance flitted to Matt’s because he had enjoyed the story of the interview when she told it in the coffee shop.

“Since I have some work to do and I’ve already heard this account, I think I’ll be going now,” he said as he rose from the chair. He stepped close to Mrs. Holmes and lightly brushed her cheek with a kiss as he squeezed her hand. “I’ll see you later. Call me if you need anything,” he directed before stepping away.

“Thank you, Mathew,” she answered with a sweet smile. “You boys take such good care of me.”

“Well, you’ve taken care of us for years. Now it’s our turn,” he replied. As he turned to leave, he noted a twinkle in Ashley’s eye. “I’ll see you later, too?” he asked hopefully.

She nodded slightly and then with an impish smile she quietly said, “Don’t I get a kiss, too?”

Without thinking, he stepped close to Ashley where she had remained seated, and simultaneously captured her hand with a light squeeze while placing a whispered kiss to her cheek. In the following seconds, Ashley found herself watching the retreating form of Matt as he hurried out of the house. He didn’t look back; he didn’t say anything; he had simply blushed and left.

When Ashley swung her gaze back to the hostess, she realized that Mrs. Holmes was speculating on the relationship between Matt and Ashley. The wrinkled weathered face was serene but mischief danced in the old woman’s ghostly silver-gray eyes. “We are just friends,” Ashley asserted staunchly.

Mrs. Holmes smiled and lifted her knitting from the basket beside her chair. But she didn’t comment.

Ashley felt her face flaming as the need to define the relationship rose within her. “We are just friends. Matt helped me the night of the wedding – when I fell. He took me to the hospital and now we are friends. I don’t know that many people around town,” she explained. “We are just friends,” she reiterated.

“Well it’s a good thing that you are,” Mrs. Holmes replied as she looked up from her knitting. “I would hope you don’t go around asking for kisses from casual acquaintances.” The landlady was teasing, Ashley was sure, but there was a hint of censure in her voice as well.

“Certainly not,” Ashley replied as she felt the rising indignation. Did Mrs. Holmes think she was a person with low morals? “In fact, I’ve rarely been kissed,” she revealed as she drew herself up and prepared to retreat to her own apartment.

"We should talk a bit more. That is, if you have the time?" the older lady said quietly without looking up. "I've been renting that apartment out for years and I've seen a lot of young people in my time. Sometimes I can help them on their journey," she continued to speak as she concentrated on her knitting. When she glanced Ashley's way, her face was kind and she said, "Don't be afraid to accept help."

Settling back into her chair, Ashley replied, "I don't need help. I need my memory back, so I can get back to my job – my life." Ashley liked visiting with her landlady. They had enjoyed several thought-provoking discussions in the days since she had moved into the apartment. And now she felt another educational lesson was in the offering, if she just opened her mind and listened.

"They aren't synonymous, you know," the older woman commented as she concentrated on her knitting.

Feeling that she had missed something vital in the exchange, Ashley rubbed her forehead. "What? What aren't synonymous?"

"You said, 'My job – my life.' They aren't the same. Your job doesn't define you," she said gently. "Your job is what you do. Your life is who you are. And God made you so much more than simply a summary of what you do." She paused and watched Ashley intently. "Be careful that the one of lesser importance doesn't overtake the one of greater importance."

"I'm going back to my life," Ashley reasserted. "I loved my job and I want to keep doing it. I just wish I could remember what happened. Why would I have quit a job that I loved?"

"It's hard to guess the answer to that mystery," Mrs. Holmes noted quietly. "Are you going to do some digging and see what you find out, or are you just going to wait for the answer to come to you?"

"I haven't decided what to do," Ashley responded. "Shelby suggested that I pray for patience and believe that God will lead me to the path He wants me on, but …" She lowered her gaze as she realized the rest of the thought: *That's not what I want.* "All I want is to go back to my career," she added sadly.

"Did you have big plans? I mean for your career?" the kind old woman asked.

"Plans? Not really. I just enjoy what I do. I mean I *enjoyed* what I *did*," she replied. "The research was interesting. And the travel was exciting." She paused and thought a moment before adding, "The pay was good, too."

"Ah. That's important, isn't it?" Mrs. Holmes said quietly. Then seeming to change the subject, she asked, "What did you think of Catherine and the job at the Chronicle?"

"Catherine?" Ashley echoed as she thought. "Catherine seems like an extremely nice lady. Very old fashioned. Trusting and sweet." She shifted her position and leaned closer to her companion as if conspiring. "Would you believe she didn't even interview me? She didn't even want to see any samples of my work. She said that Shelby's recommendation was enough and hired me right away."

"And you find that unusual?" Mrs. Holmes prodded. "Why?"

"Well, it just isn't the way people do things. There's usually a lot of competition for jobs; and backstabbing for promotions," Ashley responded as her mind flitted to the others who would like to take her spot on the research team. "To hire someone out of the blue seems … well, crazy. And dangerous." She scowled for a moment before continuing, "What if I was a criminal or something? She just hired me on nothing but Shelby's say-so."

"I suppose there's a chance that she could make a mistake about someone, but Catherine's pretty sharp," the landlady replied. "It's hard to fool her."

An image of the man at the newspaper office – Neal – came to mind and without thinking Ashley spoke. "What about Neal?"

"What about him?" Mrs. Holmes asked. "Is there a problem?" Those silvery-gray eyes focused keenly upon Ashley and she squirmed slightly under the scrutiny.

"I guess … probably not," she replied at length. "It's just that he seems angry. I mean – on the surface, he's cordial, but I feel like he's seething inside."

The gnarled hands stilled briefly, pausing from the knitting. The two women regarded each other silently for a moment until, seemingly taking on a new topic, Mrs. Holmes asked, "You said you've traveled extensively?"

"Yes."

"You enjoy it?"

Ashley nodded. Where was this conversation going?

"You meet new people all the time, right?" the elder asked.

"Well … yes." Ashley's confusion showed in her scowl. "Why are you asking?"

"Catherine hasn't traveled much for the last several years. She may have lost some of her ability to read people," the older woman answered. "But you make instant assessments on new acquaintances almost daily, right?"

"Right. I did."

"If your instincts are telling you that something is amiss, you are more than likely correct," she explained. "You have to watch yourself around Neal. And you have to take care of Catherine, too."

Ashley nodded. Mrs. Holmes' words sounded like a compliment, but also like a directive. *Watch out for yourself and Catherine, too.* "I don't know what I can do. I'm limited to part-time, plus it's temporary."

Mrs. Holmes shifted before asking, "What does Catherine have you doing?"

"I'll find out tomorrow. Probably some local resident features. Nothing too in-depth or serious, since I don't know my plans," Ashley said thoughtfully.

"Ah, yes. You have to get back to your life," Mrs. Holmes said with quiet censure in her voice. "The Bible reminds us, 'Do not boast of yourself and tomorrow, for you know not what a day may bring forth,'" she added. "Are you sure your plan and God's plan are in alignment?"

"I did have absolute confidence in my course. Thank you." Ashley's answer sounded abrupt, even to her own ears. Feeling bad for being snippy, she reached for the other woman's hand as she added, "I'm sorry, Mrs. Holmes. I didn't mean to be short with you. It's just that … well, sometimes you sound as if you think I've moved to Miller's Bend for good, but in reality, I'm just passing through."

"I was very much like you when I was younger. Much younger," the woman said with a laugh. "I was a pioneer. I worked and saved and went off to college, which was a relatively rare endeavor in my day. Most of my friends were picking out potential husbands and dreaming of homes filled with children, but not me. Oh, no. I had big plans for myself," she said quietly.

Mrs. Holmes seemed to forget about Ashley as her mind drifted back to her own younger years. "I didn't want to stay here in Miller's Bend. Washing clothes and going to Ladies Aid meetings, bearing babies and cooking and cleaning … I wanted excitement and more. I wanted to go places and see things. My plans revolved around me – me and what I wanted," she said. "I didn't listen to my parents, my friends, my teachers, or even my conscience. I wanted what I wanted, and I wouldn't be swayed."

There was a long pause before Ashley spoke. "But you went? And you succeeded?"

Ashley's comment drew the landlady's attention back to her guest. Tightening her expression and nodding affirmatively, Mrs. Holmes confirmed, "You bet I went." Then she continued somewhat sadly, "I went and I fought to get the education I wanted and then I fought to get a job in my field. And then I fought some more to keep my job and get advancements. And I won in that area. But I lost in the important areas."

Mrs. Holmes explained, "It was a difficult time for women. When I was a child, during World War II, women had moved into the workforce, but when the war ended, they were expected to step down from their positions and go back to pretending to be June Cleaver – wash and wax, cook and clean, wait on the family." When she paused, Ashley wasn't certain whether it was to compose herself or for dramatic affect.

"I was younger than those women, but I watched them. I was young and idealistic. And naïve," Mrs. Holmes continued. "I wanted to break that mold. I wanted to prove that women could be successful outside the parameters of being a wife and mother."

"That's good," Ashley answered. "Without women like you, women today would be stuck. We wouldn't be able to have meaningful careers. I wouldn't be able to be a researcher and travel the world. I would be stuck at home," she said.

"Maybe. But maybe you wouldn't have been conditioned to look at it as being 'stuck at home'. Maybe you would have been taught to view raising your children and keeping your home, loving your husband, as meaningful. Because those are valuable, rewarding undertakings as well," Mrs. Holmes countered. "There are great benefits to living small and loving fully."

"I suppose that could be true …" Ashley replied slowly as she considered the idea. "So what happened? I mean with your career – how did it all turn out?"

With the wave of a hand, Mrs. Holmes announced, "I'm afraid we'll have to finish up another time. I need to start getting ready to go to the Red Hatters meeting this afternoon."

"Alright," Ashley replied as she rose from the love seat. "I enjoyed our talk. And I think I'll do some digging this afternoon to see if I can figure out what I had planned when I quit my job."

Mrs. Holmes rose from her chair as well. She lightly touched Ashley's arm as she spoke, "As you are doing your digging, remember to try to listen for God's direction in your life. It's easier going if you're on the right path."

Two hours later, the winter wind buffeted Ashley as she stood on the patio outside the hall that had been the site of the wedding reception. Remembering the relative warmth of the sun's rays as she had walked to the Chronicle that morning, and contrasting the quick change in the weather, she marveled at how fast conditions can be transformed.

Her life had been altered by the revelation that she'd left her job where she'd been happy and comfortable; now she had to stop wandering around in limbo and start making tracks down a new path. But she really didn't want to do that. She wanted to cling to the old life.

"Tell me again why we are here," Shelby demanded through chattering teeth as she scowled at Ashley. "It's got to be below zero out here!" Turning her back to a blast of winter wind, she waited for her friend to reply.

"I'm trying to get my memory back," Ashley answered impatiently. "I told you that."

"How's this helping?"

Ashley sighed. "Well I thought if I came back to the reception hall and the patio where I fell, maybe it would 'jar something loose' in my mind," she said as she tapped a gloved finger to her temple.

"I think you 'jarred something loose' when you fell," she countered with a smile. "But … nothing's coming to you?" Shelby guessed as she took in her friend's frustrated expression.

"Nothing," she confirmed. Ashley slid down to sit on the cold concrete approximately where she guessed she had landed the night of the wedding. She leaned her head back against the wall and closed her eyes.

"You know … I don't think you can force your memory to come back," Shelby said quietly. "You'll just have to wait for God to heal you –"

"I don't want to wait!" Ashley interrupted as she snapped her head forward and opened her eyes again. "I want my memory back, so I can have my life back!"

"I don't think it works to try to order Him around like that," Shelby offered quietly. "You may think you know what you want and where you are going and when, but God might have something else entirely in mind for you."

"I'm going back East," Ashley declared as she looked up at Shelby.

Shelby smiled. "Do you have any idea how foolish you look sitting there like that?" The two burst into laughter as Shelby helped her friend to her feet. "You may just have to accept staying here for a while."

"I need to go back to my apartment. I'll have to pack up my things and ship them … somewhere. I'd guess that I gave notice before I came out here for the wedding," Ashley lamented. "Maybe I'll find something in my old apartment that will tell me what my plan was when I resigned."

"I'll see if I can arrange to go with you to keep you company and help with the packing," Shelby offered. She slipped an arm around her friend and steered her toward the car. "You should ship your belongings here," Shelby asserted as they walked across the parking lot. "Riley's parents have a place in the country. There's a shed that has plenty of space for you to store your things until you settle on a course."

"Thanks, Shel," Ashley replied. "That'd be great."

When they slid inside the car, Shelby revved the engine and turned the heater to high. "I just feel so lost," Ashley said quietly.

"Maybe 'free' is a better word for what you feel," Shelby countered.

"Free?"

"Free to try something new. Free to change directions," she explained. "Free."

"I don't want to try something new or change directions," Ashley stated. She spoke very clearly, "I want to go back to my life. That's what I want."

"It might not be what God wants for you."

"I don't care!"

Shelby raised her eyebrows as she regarded her friend with surprise. "Since when do you not care what God wants?"

CHAPTER FIVE

"Missing children?" Ashley echoed the words Catherine had spoken with quiet authority in the private office of the Chronicle. "You believe young people from this area are being taken?" Ashley's voice quavered slightly with disbelief, but at the same time she felt an adrenaline surge. Could there really be a story that big in the tiny little town? "Or are they simply runaways?"

"Maybe." Catherine's reply was a bit raspy. "I don't think they are being transported out of the country, but young, vulnerable girls are being persuaded to leave their families," she explained. "Someone is recruiting them out of small rural communities – this one in particular – and in some cases, they never contact their loved ones again."

Ashley considered what she was hearing. She had expected her freelance work for the Chronicle to be easy little fluff pieces, but this story might actually be challenging. And meaningful. Her heart rate picked up as she realized her investigative skills would be put to use. "Where do I start?" she asked the older woman.

"I've made a list of local characters that I'd like you to write feature stories about," Catherine replied, seeming to have dropped the idea of the community's lost young women altogether. She rifled through piles of manila file folders stacked chaotically on her desk while Ashley waited for this encounter to make sense.

Concerned because of the confusion she asked again, "What am I to write for the Chronicle?"

"Listen carefully," her boss said as she pulled a file folder to her chest. The woman's bright blue eyes sparkled as they locked with Ashley's. "Go and interview each of the people I have listed here. Do nice easy feature stories. Stories about their hobbies, their collections, their careers – whatever you find that is interesting to the local readers," she paused and cleared her throat before continuing. "But always, always be looking for components of the other story. The one we just talked about. Don't mention it; don't bring it up; don't tell anyone that is what you are really working on. Do you understand?"

Ashley's mind was full of questions, but the headache was beginning to set in again. She reached for the folder and nodded. "These are the families who lost their daughters?" she asked to confirm that she understood correctly.

The front door of the newspaper building had opened and closed. They were no longer alone. Catherine glanced toward the front room before confirming with an animated nod. But her verbal response gave no indication of the covert story she had asked for. "Just do nice easy features on these people, so I can get a feel for your writing style …," she directed in a clear voice designed to carry throughout the building. She lowered the volume before adding, "Before the transition."

"Why haven't you …" Ashley began to ask, but was silenced when Catherine grabbed her uninjured wrist.

"I'm too close to the people involved," she whispered. "But I'm warning you. It's not safe to discuss this with anyone. Understand?"

"What transition?" Ashley asked awkwardly. Her mind had snagged on the words Catherine had spoken quietly.

The old woman's expression was that of a person indulging a child when she responded, "Oh, you know: the transition. We'll talk more about it later."

Neal, the Chronicle's news reporter, returned to the office from wherever he'd been, just as Catherine finished clarifying Ashley's assignment. Ashley returned to the desk that was designated as her work space. She slipped the folder into her bag and pulled the laptop out to settle it on the desk. She hoped Neal hadn't noticed the folder, but he probably had. Something about the guy gave Ashley the creeps.

Sitting with her back to her temporary coworker, she opened the screen on her laptop, using it as a mirror so she could see Neal. She was surprised to find an almost sinister image glaring toward her. Ashley supposed he was worried that she would be in some sort of competition with him, but that wasn't her intention at all. Intending to reassure him, she swiveled her chair to face him with a smile.

"Well, newbie," he began in a slightly patronizing tone. "I suppose you have first day jitters … I'd be happy to help you understand how things work around here." He stood and paced toward Ashley until he was too close and towering over her.

At 26, Ashley wasn't exactly wet behind the ears. She'd grown up in a tough metro area of the Twin Cities and she'd been a researcher for a major news network. She'd traveled extensively in inhospitable conditions, and she could recognize a bully without any additional prompting. And Neal most definitely was a bully. Oh, he was highly educated and well dressed, but he was trying to manipulate Ashley and she'd never responded well to that.

Pushing to her feet, she rose to stand toe-to-toe with Neal, ready to meet any confrontation. Her movement had forced him to step back, which had been her intent. Once they were both standing and Ashley had reclaimed her psychological territory she spoke quietly but very clearly as she met his gaze. "I think I've got a handle on how things work around here," she declared. Thinking that there was no point in sparring with the man when she fully wished to be back to her real job as soon as possible, she relaxed her stance slightly and reminded him, "You do know I'm just here temporarily? I have no intention of staying in Miller's Bend, or here at the Chronicle."

"Two weeks," he said with a slight challenge. "I'll bet you can't stand the small town life for more than two weeks."

Ashley considered the statement before shrugging. "Could be," she conceded quietly. "How long have you been here?"

Neal had relaxed slightly and his focus drifted to look through the rippled glass of the front windows in the newspaper building. The building was well over 100 years old with nearly all its features original to the 1880s era. The glass wasn't clear and it wasn't high quality, giving the viewer the feeling that they were watching a dream or mirage when looking out. "Eleven years," he said with a sigh. "It's been eleven years since we moved to Miller's Bend."

"Who's we?" Ashley asked tentatively. She didn't really like this coworker, but thought getting to know him better might improve the situation. "You have a family?"

"My wife, Cheryl," he confirmed without emotion. "And we have a son. He's eight." Neal didn't look happy; he looked resigned. Ashley had grown up believing that people who were married were in love and happier than those who were single, but she'd seen enough contrary evidence over the years that she'd come to question the assumption. Looking at Neal, she guessed that he and Cheryl were one more case to disprove her youthful delusions.

Taking one final stab at friendly conversation, she asked, "What brought you to Miller's Bend from … where did you live before?"

"Cheryl's family is here and she needed to come back when her mother was in declining health," he offered half an answer. "I need to make some calls," he declared as he turned away.

Ashley settled into her chair and powered up her computer. As she waited, she swiveled toward Neal again. "Thanks for the chat," she offered pleasantly. "You know, I'm no threat to your position here."

When he looked up, she saw disgust plainly displayed across his harsh features. "My position is a joke – I'm a glorified errand boy," he said with a slight sneer. "But, I will be the editor. Catherine can't hang on much longer."

The tingles that Ashley had come to associate with danger tripped up her spine. Warnings buzzed in her mind. Mrs. Holmes' directive to watch out for Catherine resurfaced and Ashley was careful to hide her rising suspicions as she asked, "Has there been some kind of trouble?"

Neal pulled his lips back in a way that reminded Ashley of a canine about to growl in order to assert its dominance. "Nothing I can't fix when I'm in charge." He stood and strode purposefully toward Catherine's office. Ashley watched in stunned amazement as he retreated. Had she misunderstood, or was Neal on the offensive to drive Catherine and Charlie out of their business?

Turning back to her computer, she began her research into the background information on missing children, runaways and human trafficking. Engrossed in her work, Ashley was surprised when lunchtime rolled around. Glancing at the clock on the wall she confirmed what her stomach had been trying to tell her – definitely time for a break. She closed her laptop and grabbed her bag as she headed out to the little coffee shop where she and Matt had visited the day before. She went straight to the counter to place her order and when she turned to look for an open table, she discovered they were all taken.

She noted a table where a lone patron sat with his back to her. Perhaps he wouldn't mind some company. As she drew near, she sensed something familiar about him … and then he turned his head … Matt. Her breath caught and she stopped. Pushing his chair back he turned and stood, "Hi, Ashley," he said quietly. "Join me?" he invited as he indicated the chair across the table from his own.

"Yes, thank you."

"How's the first day at your new job?" he asked casually. Matt's crystal blue eyes seemed to hold Ashley in a trance as he watched her.

Finally the words registered and she felt the need to refute the implication. "It's not my new job. I'm just freelancing for a while," she clarified.

He nodded. "Until you get your memory back. I remember," he confirmed. "How's your first day at your freelance not-job?" he asked again with humor.

She smiled in return and relaxed. At least one person understood that she had no plans to stay in Miller's Bend. "It's kind of … odd," she said, thinking of the secret assignment and her strange temporary coworker. "What do you know about Neal?"

Matt grimaced. "I don't know … they live kind of … differently. He seems nice, but really superficial," he said. "It's like you don't know who he really is or what he's thinking."

"Oh, I know what he's thinking!" Ashley replied too quickly. And then when Matt looked disapprovingly at her, she became defensive. "He told me straight out that he doesn't like his job, but he plans on taking over the newspaper. He said, 'Catherine can't hold on much longer.'"

"He told you that?" Matt asked with suspicion. "Why would he tell you? If it's true, why would he tell anyone?"

"He was trying to assert himself over me," she replied. "I told him not to worry about me. I'll be moving on." She paused to consider the circumstances before continuing, "I think that once he was sure I won't be around he thought he would help push me along."

"Well, it won't matter to you anyway," Matt said as he gave her a long look. "You'll be gone. I'm sure he'll learn the business quickly enough." He wasn't sure why, but the idea that she'd be leaving Miller's Bend bothered him. Maybe he was just getting tired of everybody leaving.

"What do you mean … he'll learn the business? He said he's been here eleven years?" Ashley asked. Her curiosity rose quickly, along with concern for the small-town newspaper and its owners, Catherine and Charlie. "Surely he knows the business by now?"

"He hasn't been here that long … I think it's more like two years. And, as far as I know, he's only been with the paper since Shelby quit when she had the babies," he supplied. "He doesn't know much about journalism."

Ashley stared at the man across the table from her with confusion. "Why would he want to take over the newspaper if it isn't what he's trained for? And by the way, what is he trained for?"

Again, Matt shrugged. "I'm not positive, but I think he's had some training in psychology. Or maybe it was sociology. I really don't remember," he contributed. Matt looked away, across the busy dining area, and when his focus returned to Ashley, he spoke sullenly, "Could we maybe discuss something other than Neal?"

Ashley thought for a moment as she chewed and swallowed a bite of her lunch which had been silently delivered to the table midway through the conversation. Matt had finished eating and seemed content to stay while she ate. Finally, she mentioned a statistic that she had discovered in her morning research, "Did you know it's estimated that each year there are between 1.3 and 1.5 million runaway and homeless youth in the United States?"

Matt stiffened in his chair, his focus snapping toward Ashley, "Why would you mention that?" He watched her coldly for a minute until she responded.

"What's the matter? You said you wanted to talk about something else …" she replied. "I was doing some research this morning and I came across that statistic. I just thought it would be interesting."

"Interesting?" he growled as he shot a stony glare across the table.

"Well, yes," she answered as bewilderment set in. He looked angry … angry at her. But, she thought that forging ahead would be better than turning back. "Did you know that in North America, runaway youth are widely regarded as a chronic and serious social problem?"

"They are not 'social problems' and they are more than statistics!" he hissed. "They are children and young girls who are missing. Their families don't know if they are alive or dead. Families don't know if they've been abused or victimized or if by God's grace they are safe. And for every missing child, there are whole families whose lives stop while they search, and hope and pray for their safety. And for their return."

Ashley's face burned with embarrassment and shame. She'd been trying to just visit with the man, but apparently she'd hit a hot button and set him off. People were looking their way, and much of the background noise in the little coffee shop had ground to a stop. "I'm sorry, Matt," she said quietly. "It's just that I was researching and I like to talk about what I learn. It helps lock it in my memory."

He continued to glare. "We are not talking about runaways," he declared with deceptive quietness.

"Okay. Okay," she sighed. "No runaways and no talking about whoever you lost …" She let the sentence trail away as she regarded him a moment. Questions began to form in her mind, but she stifled them. He owed her no explanations. "I'm sorry. I didn't mean to upset you," she offered after a long pause.

Matt's agitation hadn't abated, but Ashley could tell that he was trying to relax and refocus. "Maybe I should just go back to work," she suggested.

"Just wait," he requested. "I'll try to behave." His smile was a little forced, but it was back, as he reached forward and touched Ashley's hand.

"Alright. But you have to pick the next topic. Agreed?" she replied and returned a smile.

"Agreed," he confirmed with a nod. "So, have you seen Shelby lately?"

A snort escaped from Ashley before she could stop it.

"What's that mean?" he asked as his smile faded. "Is there trouble?"

"She's a little peeved at me," Ashley responded. Pulling her tumbles of red hair back over her shoulders and dropping the length of it down her back, she shrugged. "It's my fault. I said some stupid things."

"I'm sure she'll forgive you," he assured her confidently. "She's kind of that way."

"Will you forgive me?" she asked. "I seem to have said some stupid things to you, too."

Taking her hand in his, he examined it for a few seconds before raising his focus to her face. He pulled up a sad smile and replied, "Of course. I can't seem to stay angry with anyone. It's just not in my nature."

Glancing at her cell phone, she was surprised to see the time. "I'd better run. I've got two interviews lined up this afternoon," she said apologetically. "I'd like to talk some more … when I haven't upset you …"

"Me too," Matt answered with a real smile this time. He stood to pull her chair back and helped Ashley into her jacket. "I haven't seen your portfolio … maybe you want to bring it by my place Friday around six? We could have supper and then I could see some of your work," he suggested.

She didn't answer right away. And then with the color rising in his cheeks, he looked away, "Unless you have plans …"

Sadness tugged at her. She didn't want to hurt his feelings, but she did have other plans for Friday evening. "Actually, I do," she said. Matt tried to hold his expression neutral, but Ashley noticed the slight droop to his shoulders and disappointment in his eyes. Before thinking, she quickly added, "But we could do it the next Friday. I mean … if that works for you?"

His smile bloomed as he registered her answer. "Yah. Yes. That's perfect!"

Ashley's heart raced and her mind warned her that this sounded like a date. She shouldn't go. She should say she had other plans. She should make other plans. And when she opened her mouth, the words rolled out, “Sounds great! I’ll see you then -”

Matt told her the directions to his home, rather than a street address, as he escorted her back to the office door of the Chronicle. As he departed with a quick smile and a wave, she thought how different it must be, living in a small town where people can find each other by going two blocks west of the water tower, hanging a left and looking for a white ranch-style house which can’t possibly be missed.

CHAPTER SIX

Matt tuned the sound system in the studio to a local Christian music station and he hummed along as his hands molded the clay. He had previously completed sketches of the new multiple-piece sculpture he was commissioned to create. With prayerful consideration he had let the pieces develop in a series of drawings, and then proceeded to meet with the board that hired him. After getting the group's approval on the designs, he was ready to begin the process of developing the first of the images on the paper into a three-dimensional creation in clay.

Even though he had phoned his mother to be sure she was alright before he could settle in to work for several hours, he was concerned about her. She'd cheerfully informed him that he worried too much. "Go ahead and get some work done," she'd replied. "A friend stopped by and we're visiting. I'll be just fine."

As he began to work on the form of the sculpture, his mind leapt from one troubling topic to the next: his mom; his sister; Tyler's words … Had Matt's actions contributed to Chrissi's need to run? And why was Tyler concerned?; Ashley's fall and memory loss; Lauren's departure from Miller's Bend; Mrs. Holmes … not that there was anything wrong with her … she just needed someone to care about her, and Ashley's new job … what had she said about Neal wanting to take over the paper?

"Ashley?" he whispered to himself. "How did she get in the list twice?" He shook his head as if to clear his thinking. "How did she get in there at all?"

He stood to stretch his muscles, walked over to the kitchenette to get himself a drink and lowered his head. He pictured Ashley the night of the wedding reception – there had been something about her that drew his attention, even before she was injured in the fall. He remembered the way she had looked to him with her dazzling blue eyes full of confusion, but trusted him to take care of her. He'd spoken with her a couple more times since she'd been released from the hospital, and they seemed to have an instant sense of camaraderie. The thought that he'd invited her to supper Friday rose up in his mind. Why had he done it? He didn't want to grow closer to her. Ashley would take her bright smile, her intriguing sense of humor, red hair and dimples, along with her worldly ways, and return to her exciting life on the leading edge of the news reporting world. He'd cared for enough people who had left … why attach himself to another?

But maybe – just maybe – she wouldn't leave. Ashley said that she had quit her job, although she didn't remember doing it or why. Maybe she was ready to make the leap to a new life, a different lifestyle. Maybe … she needed to get her memory back. Until she reclaimed the memories that her mind had tucked away, her life was a mirage. What appeared to be wasn't necessarily fact. He decided that when they met the following Friday for supper, he would try to help her remember the night of the fall. He couldn't help with what came before that, but he would do what he could for her.

And there he stood, promising himself that he would help yet another person. He lowered his head and spoke softly, "Lord, don't you think I have enough on my plate without drawing me into whatever Ashley's issues are? I don't know if I can handle more."

He'd been so consumed by the stresses of his life that he'd been almost afraid to attempt the creative process, but he needed to. Sculpting wasn't just his livelihood, it was also his therapy. He returned to his sculpting table, and as he began to work the clay, his instincts took over and he felt at peace. Riley's words came back to him: *It's alright to accept some help. Let your friends back you up.*

The music of popular musicians repeated the messages of faith that he had embraced in his teens and relied on for years. Soon he felt the calmness that came with losing himself in the medium and the process of creating. As he continued, the sense of peace and calmness grew.

He was completely immersed in the comforting act of sculpting when the sound of a car door closing outside the studio drew his attention. Matt stood and stretched and wiped his hands before moving toward the door. He pulled his cell phone from his pocket to check the time as he crossed the studio, and was shocked to see that hours had passed since he'd settled in to work on the piece. Thinking that he'd better check on his mom as soon as the visitor left, he pulled the door open and froze.

Shock stole the words he might have spoken as Matt stared at the man who stood across the sill. In a matter of seconds, a myriad of emotions roiled through Matt. He was surprised to realize that anger wasn't among them, but hope and disappointment both were present. The man was shorter than Matt by several inches and it seemed odd to be looking down on the man he had once looked up to. "Sixteen years." The words slipped out before Matt realized he'd even formed the thought.

Signs of remorse moved across the older man's features. "Yes, Mathew. Sixteen years," he replied. "I'm sorry … But I suppose that doesn't matter. Does it?"

"Not so much," Matt replied steadily. "Why are you here, Byron?"

"You called me about Chrissi," the man replied calmly. "You look good." Neither man moved for a moment while tensions seemed to build. Matt thought of a teacher from high school who had often used the phrase, "a pregnant pause," and at last he understood. It was a brief period of time filled with potential just waiting to be released and directed. Years of hurt, longing and disappointment could pollute the moment, or the two men who loved Chrissi could work together to try to save her.

Matt swallowed hard. "You look old," he said at length. He stepped back to allow Byron to enter as he extended the invitation to come inside.

A faint smile hovered at the corners of the visitor's mouth, before he replied, "Thanks. I feel old." Byron stepped into the studio, but stayed near the door. He slowly scanned the room as he waited for Matt to speak, but the silence stretched. Finally, Byron offered quietly, "You do quality work. You've been making a name for yourself."

The pride that filled Matt's heart was quickly tempered by suspicion. "Why would you care?" And then before he could stop himself, he added an offensive barb, "And I don't need your approval." He turned away on the pretense of cleaning up, but his eyes stung. Why would this man's approval matter? Byron had only been his step-dad, and only for about three years. And he'd left.

Chrissi. Matt needed to focus on Chrissi, or he was going to embarrass himself.

"Chrissi," Matt croaked as he turned back to face Byron. "I called you because we tracked her to Boulder. I left you a message – all you had to do was call me back if she contacted you." His gaze danced around the room refusing to land on anything but Byron. In a hoarse whisper, he added, "Why are you here?"

"I need to help you find her."

"No … you don't," Matt asserted. "I'll find her. We've tracked her to Boulder; we'll pick up her trail again soon."

"She's traveling with cash and new cell phones. Using an alias," Byron spoke slowly and then waited for the information to sink in. He remembered Matt as smart and he was hoping that would override the stubbornness that the boy had embodied as well. "Chrissi is a smart woman and -"

"Chrissi is a girl!" Matt countered. "She's not a woman; she's a girl." He paced away as he muttered about nobody understanding that his little sister is not a woman. Not an adult. Not a grown up.

The muscles in Matt's neck and shoulders tensed with stress. And when he felt Byron's touch on his shoulder, he swung around to face the man who should have been there to raise them, but had bailed out and abandoned the family. He couldn't stop himself from batting Byron's hand away. "Don't! Don't try to make up now for what you should have been doing for years," Matt's frustrations pushed him to the edge and he instinctively lashed out. "We needed you *then*. We don't need you *now*."

Byron's cell phone rang and when it looked as if he would ignore it, Matt gave a hoarse laugh. "You may as well answer it. I think we're done here," he choked out. With the look of a defeated man, Byron turned away and answered the call.

As Matt watched his step-dad, Chrissi's father, it struck him that the visit was taking a toll. Matt was forced to admit that even though he'd thought Byron looked old when he first walked into the studio, the man appeared to have aged an additional ten years in the last few minutes.

Blocking out the phone conversation, Matt formed a quick prayer: *Lord, please forgive me ... I know I reacted badly, but ... what do I do? Please help me find the reactions you want from me, please guide my responses.*

"Mathew?" Byron's voice responded. The voice was quiet, soft and comforting. And the man held the cell phone in his direction. "You're mother wants to talk to you," he explained as he placed it into Matt's hand. "I'll wait outside."

With stooped shoulders and lowered head, Byron made for the exit. Matt glanced between the phone clutched in his hand and the retreating man. "Byron," he said just as the man reached for the door knob. "I'm sorry. Please stay in here."

The older man's eyes held Matt's for an assessing moment, and then he nodded.

Nodding in response, Matt slowly raised the phone. "Hi, Mom." After several minutes of listening and mumbling responses, he pushed the button to disconnect the call and handed the phone back to Byron. "She reminded me that God gave me two ears and only one mouth, so I can listen twice as much as I talk," he said with a slight smile. "She seems to think you and I can have a calm discussion."

"We'll see," Byron answered slowly. He moved closer to Matt and placed a gentle hand on his shoulder before he added, "I'm pretty sure you're going to be upset."

"I am, too."

Byron explained that he had spent the afternoon visiting with is former wife, Matt's mother, and she filled him in on the steps Matt had taken in searching for his sister. He suggested that in the interest of expediency, they should meet with Matt's lawyer and the local law enforcement before he revealed the remainder of the information he had to share. Matt made the calls and then he drove to the police station with Byron riding shotgun.

The two men rode in silence the first few blocks. Matt stopped at a red traffic light.

"Why did you leave?" Matt asked suddenly. "Why?"

The other man didn't turn to face him, but asked with a note of skepticism in his voice, "You want to get into this now?"

"The short answer," Matt replied after a second's hesitation. The light changed to green and Matt hit the accelerator.

"We had troubles and no matter how hard I tried – whatever I did – I couldn't make it work," Byron replied. When Matt glanced at Byron, he was surprised to see his stepfather's eyes revealed the shadows of years of regrets. Byron shrugged slightly and concluded simply, "I couldn't compete with her memories of your father."

A scowl darkened Matt's expression. His father had died suddenly, and almost as suddenly, Byron became part of the household. Then there had been the new baby and just when Matt started to believe that his life was stable and normal, the bottom dropped out. Byron had run off, abandoning and devastating his family. "Why did you marry her if you didn't love her? Why have a child?" Matt asked with the words sticking in his throat.

"Your dad was one of my best friends," Byron replied quietly. "He had asked me to take care of you if anything happened to him. I didn't think it would ever become a reality, but it did."

"Kind of missed the mark on that one, didn't you?" Matt snarled, as what he vowed would be the final verbal jab at his stepfather slipped past his lips. He was quickly realizing that taking shots at Byron wasn't making either of them feel better, and it wasn't helping to find Chrissi. Plus, the man looked genuinely remorseful and refused to argue. He parked the car and turned to face Byron. "Look. I'm sorry," he offered in a stilted voice. "I'm not like that," he sighed. "At least – not normally."

Byron nodded as his older, wiser expression took in Matt's distress. "I know it's a lot to deal with," he replied. "Maybe we could focus on getting Chrissi home safely? After that, we could hash out the past, if you still want to."

They entered the police offices where they met Police Chief Jeff Schuster, as well as Matt's friend and lawyer, Mason Alexander, and Sheriff Erik Dunn. The chief led the entourage through the corridor and into one of the private meeting rooms before securing the door behind them. Each man settled in one of the comfortable chairs positioned around the table. Blank notebooks lay before Jeff and Erik as they glanced between Matt and Byron expectantly. Mason pulled a thick file from his briefcase and looked to Matt to start the conversation.

With a quickly formulated prayer that God would guide his words and help them find Chrissi, Matt inhaled deeply. He looked earnestly from face to face as he began, "My sister,

Chrissi, left home about three weeks ago, and it's time that we involve the law."

"What?! She's been missing for weeks and you didn't report it?" the chief bellowed as he leaned forward in his chair, his rotund belly pushing against the table. "Are you nuts? She could have been -" He stopped himself and looked from Matt to Mason. And then with a slight accusation in his voice, narrowed his eyes, and stated, "You knew about this."

A twinge of guilt stabbed at Matt's consciousness. Chief Schuster wasn't simply the law in Miller's Bend; he was also a friend of their family. Maybe Matt should have gone to him …

"I advised that the family notify you," Mason answered calmly. "Both of you," he added as his gaze moved to include Sheriff Erik Dunn. The sheriff was young, inexperienced and had only been elected into office in November. Many talked as though they thought he was about as qualified as a middle school student would be, but Mason liked the man. He found Erik to be likable and he respected the handling of the few cases that had been processed in recent months, even though Dunn hadn't exactly been put to the test on any serious incidents as yet.

"Yes, he did," Matt confirmed with a nod. "Our mother didn't believe that Chrissi's leaving was anything to bring the law into. She was confident that Chrissi was just showing her independence and would be home soon."

"But now?" the chief prodded.

"But now …" Matt stopped speaking and swiveled his head toward Byron and gestured with a swing of his hand. "But now my … stepfather is here and he says he's seen her and has new information."

Silence reigned and then, when it appeared no one would speak, Mason cleared his throat and began, saying, "Both Matt and their mother were in contact with the young woman -"

"Girl," Matt insisted with a dark look toward his friend.

"As I was saying, they'd been in contact with Chrissi the first few days after she'd left Miller's Bend," Mason continued as he deftly ignored Matt's persistence that his sister was still a child. Handing information packets to both officers of the law, Mason reviewed the information he had. "Chrissi didn't appear to be trying to hide her absence from her family, but she wouldn't reveal her destination or reasons for leaving."

"You spoke with her?" the young sheriff asked. He'd been listening intently and reading the facial expressions and body language of those present.

"Yes, I spoke with her," Matt confirmed. "I knew she was planning some kind of adventure and I confronted her about her plans before she left."

"Why didn't you stop her from going? Ground her? Take away her privileges?" the sheriff asked with rising concern. "A minor child –" He stopped abruptly when he noticed Jeff shaking his head. "What?" he demanded.

"Chrissi isn't one to be deterred easily," the older lawman replied as he leaned back in his chair. "She's headstrong, alright."

"And she's no minor," Mason added with a dark look toward Matt. "Regardless of her brother's delusions, she's 18 and doesn't exactly have to obey him." Matt sent an icy glare toward his friend in response to the statement.

"We have to find her," Matt declared. "Byron asked me to get you all together. He has information that will help."

Byron, who had been silently taking in the exchange, nodded slowly before he began to speak. “I’m pretty sure she’s in the Chicago area,” he began.

CHAPTER SEVEN

The phone lay on the vanity and, as Ashley finished applying her makeup, she listened to the disembodied voice of her father through the speaker. She sighed as he told her to look for the good in her new situation. She'd been taught all her life to look for the silver lining, even when the rain clouds hovered in her life. With exasperation, she asked, "What's the silver lining, Dad? I can't see it."

She heard the humor in his voice as Chuck replied, "Just because you can't see it yet, doesn't mean it isn't there. Remember to give thanks in all circumstances."

Slipping into a soft, cream colored sweater, Ashley replied. "Give thanks for what?"

"I don't know," he answered. Gently he added, "A chance for a fresh start, a place to live, a job, friends … If you try, I think you'll appreciate what you have."

Feeling the sting of the mild rebuke, Ashley nodded. Of course, her father couldn't see the gesture so she picked up the phone. "Thanks, Daddy. I got mired down in focusing on things I've lost and didn't look for the blessings I have."

"It'll all work out, honey," Ashley's father assured her. "You can always come home for a while if you need to. You know that."

Ashley laughed, feeling her spirit lightening. "I know I can, Daddy. But I'd prefer not to come home. I'm alright for the time being."

"I'd better let you go. It's Friday night and you've probably got plans?" he asked.

She replied with a sound of agreement before adding, "Allison and Andrew are picking me up, and we'll meet Shelby and Riley for dinner. So, I do need to finish getting ready."

"Alright. I love you," he replied.

"Love you, too."

They ended the call shortly before Allison and Andrew, who had returned from their honeymoon, picked Ashley up to meet Riley and Shelby at a local supper club. Ashley had been looking forward to an evening with her friends. She expected the brothers would leave the girls alone to visit, but that's not at all the way the evening turned out. At the table, Ashley found herself seated next to a man her friends had mentioned, but she had no memory of ever having met, Mason Alexander. And, she was seated directly across from Matt. Allison was beside Ashley with Andrew on her other side. Rounding out the gathering were Shelby and Riley, and Tyler Schuster.

Conversation flowed, and Ashley found that the circle of friends seemed deeply interwoven, and she felt a pang of regret that she was an outsider – a guest, but not really belonging. Her work had left her with few personal ties as she moved from location to location. Other than her long friendships with Shelby and Allison, she'd been content with superficial relationships with her coworkers, but the closeness of this group of people had her wondering if she wasn't missing out on something important in her own life. The option of staying in Miller's Bend would certainly give her the opportunity to settle down and develop friendships and relationships with people like those at the table.

Ashley glanced at the faces around the table. Her two best friends in the world, and their spouses, were there; as well as Mason, Matt and Tyler. "I've got news," she began when there was a break in the conversation.

"Your memory?" Allison asked quickly. Ashley noted that Matt was watching her intently with a hopeful expression. She didn't want to disappoint them, but her memory still hadn't returned.

Shaking her head, she answered, "No." And then perking up she revealed, "But I have made a decision." She paused a second as she took in the expectant gazes of her friends. "I've been kind of … surly … toward some of you, and I'm sorry. It's just difficult, this feeling that I'm adrift without my recent memories. But I've decided to try to focus on the present and the future, rather than what I've lost or left behind. I've chosen to move beyond it."

"What are you trying to tell us? What is it?" Shelby queried impatiently.

"I've decided to stay in Miller's Bend and give this path a chance to work out for me," Ashley declared. She nodded firmly, adding emphasis to her statement, and causing her red curls to cascade around her shoulders. She cast her gaze around the table, seeing approval in everyone's faces.

There was a pause, and Allison wrapped her in a quick hug, there was squealing, probably from Shelby. Supportive words - "That's great," "Good for you," "Was there any question?" flowed around the table. But it was Matt's reaction that Ashley honed in on. He didn't say anything. He just watched her. His eyes shone and a huge smile broke across his face and his gaze held hers and finally he mouthed the words quietly, "I'm glad."

It was then that Ashley realized *she* was glad she was staying, too. She reflected on Mrs. Holmes' words: *Your job doesn't define you. Your job is what you do. Your life is who you are.* Ashley felt as if she was beginning to come back to herself. The absence of memories from the weeks prior to her fall wasn't nearly as consuming as it had been. Ashley realized that she'd begun to look forward; to move forward and to embrace a new job. She wasn't a new person, just a person with a new outlook.

Her gaze snagged on Matt's until, belatedly, she realized that Mason had slipped an arm across the back of her chair and touched her shoulder. Ashley glanced toward him, as he added quietly, "I'd like to be the first to officially welcome you to town."

Oddly embarrassed by the gesture and comment, Ashley whispered a thank you before quickly lowering her gaze. She shifted forward in the chair, and looked to Matt, thinking she would ask him if he would advise her about looking for a vehicle to purchase. But when she turned to him, he'd turned away and seemed to be listening intently to a story Tyler was relating. There was obvious tension in his jaw and the skin above his collar had reddened, as though he was suppressing an irritation.

She turned her attention instead to Allison who was talking about how nice the honeymoon trip had been, and how she looked forward to settling in to their new life as a family. Ashley listened as the conversations flowed. She was happy.

A cover band began playing in the banquet room and the sounds of revelers filtered through to the dining area. When the meal concluded and the conversation slowed, the couples slipped away from the table to go dancing. As Ashley watched them moving toward the dance floor, Mason drew her attention with a slight clearing of his throat. She glanced toward him as he pushed back from the table and rose, extending a hand to her. "May I have this dance, milady?" he asked with polished grace.

Ashley felt a smile bloom as she looked up into his expectant gaze. "You're not from here, are you?" she queried.

"Let's dance and we can discuss it," he replied gently. A waggle of his bold eyebrows, elicited a laugh from Ashley as she accepted his hand. "If you'll excuse us, gentlemen," Mason directed toward their tablemates. She rose gracefully and as Mason stepped behind her, placing his hand at her back to guide her through the maze of tables, she glanced back at Tyler and Matt. Tyler had leaned toward Matt, deep in storytelling mode, but Matt's eyes were tracking her retreat from the dining room.

She paused, curious about Matt's interest in her and Mason. She would rather dance with Matt, but he hadn't asked. And besides, there was that strange fascination she had with him – probably best if they keep some distance. Mason stopped beside Ashley. "Something wrong?" he asked quietly.

Flashing a quick glance back at the table, Ashley saw that Matt had turned his attention to Tyler's story. "No. Nothing," she answered when she raised her focus to Mason's face.

Matt tried to listen to Tyler's story, but his mind continuously carried him back to the time he had spent with Ashley. The vulnerable woman he had helped the night of the wedding, taking her to the hospital, had disappeared. In her place, Matt noticed the strong, smart, funny woman who had emerged. Despite missing her memories of the preceding weeks, she was more than equipped to take care of herself, while still caring about others. She was naturally curious and kind and giving.

And Matt was attracted by her – attracted *to* her. As Ashley and Mason had begun winding their way among the diners to reach the dance floor, Matt hadn't been able to make himself look away until she glanced back at him. He wanted to take her dancing. He longed to hold her in his arms. And he wondered what it would be like to kiss her …

"… go after her," Tyler's voice broke into Matt's consciousness, causing him to jerk back to the conversation at hand.

"You should definitely go after her," Tyler repeated slowly as though he was deep in thought. "I think she's in trouble."

Matt considered the way Ashley had hesitated before moving away from the table with Mason before answering his friend. With a shake of his head he said quietly, "She'll be fine. There's nothing I can do."

Tyler's incredulous stare had Matt wondering which one of them was off-track. Matt suspected it was himself because he hadn't really been listening. His thoughts had been centered on Ashley gliding toward the dance floor where Mason would wrap her in his arms, hold her close and …. Matt dropped his fists to the table, making the glasses and dishes rattle.

The confused look in Tyler's eyes transformed as he glanced toward the dance floor. Anger flashed in his silver eyes. "*I* was talking about *Chrissi*," he said hotly. "You know – your little sister – the one nobody has heard from in weeks!"

Chrissi. Of course. Matt had actually been thinking the same thing … that he should go get her and bring her home. And, of course he would do just that, as soon as the Chicago, or where ever she was, police notified Sheriff Dunn of her location. Byron had brought news about Chrissi and they had worked together with the chief of police, Tyler's father and family friend, and with the new sheriff. Matt's mom had originally thought that Chrissi was just spreading her wings, and they should give her room and time. But as the days turned to weeks, his mother finally agreed that it was time to go after Chrissi.

He worried about her and prayed for her safety. The reaction Ashley's comments about runaways had sparked from Matt confirmed the possibility he hadn't allowed himself to consider – that Chrissi had run away from them. Worse yet, what if something bad happened to her? It was his responsibility to take care of her. That's what he'd been told from the time she was born. Matt knew in his heart that he would have to go after her and bring her back to Miller's Bend. Her time of spreading her wings was over.

But Matt had other responsibilities, too. And he couldn't just take off and ignore those. Maybe he was going to need help finding his sister. Or maybe he needed help caring for his mother. Maybe. Maybe he would have to let his friends help.

"You know she's a headstrong girl," Matt finally answered his friend as he pulled his gaze away from the dance floor. "She won't appreciate being dragged home. And she probably wouldn't stay put after I got her here."

"She's a woman, Matt. And something's wrong. I just have a feeling that she's gotten herself into trouble of some kind," Tyler said as he studied something on a far wall. Without looking back to his friend, he added, "I think we need to go after her." He stood and strode purposefully away from the table leaving Matt alone.

We? We should go after her?

Mason and Ashley danced a couple of lively dances and when the first strains of a slow song came up, Ashley hesitated to move into Mason's arms. "It's okay. I assure you I am a gentleman," he said reassuringly. Taking him at his word, Ashley stepped closer and they began to sway with the music.

"So you were going to tell me where you are from," she prompted.

"Ah, yes," Mason replied in an exaggerated Southern accent. "You've deciphered that I'm an immigrant to the plains?"

"Indeed," Ashley replied with a faux British accent. "From whence do you hail?"

"Why, I was born and raised in the fine state of Georgia, Ma'am," he replied with pride. And then dropping the accent, he continued, "Andrew and I became friends in college."

"Ah."

"Ah?" he echoed.

"How did you get to Miller's Bend?"

"I drove," he replied easily as they maneuvered around the dance floor. "The airport isn't finished yet and I didn't want to hop a freight train."

Smiling again, Ashley advised, "You know, if you find yourself unemployed, you may have a future in comedy."

When the song ended, the two returned to the table only to find Matt sitting alone. Again, as she had the day they stopped at the coffee shop, Ashley was struck with the sense that Matt had suffered a great loss and her heart urged her to reach out to him. He glanced up, meeting her gaze briefly before sighing as he rose. "I'm heading for home," he declared as he got up from his chair, stepped back and turned away.

"Wait." The word had slipped from Ashley's lips before she realized it had formed. Matt paused and looked back over his shoulder, but didn't respond. She continued, "Can you give me a lift back to Mrs. Holmes' place, please?"

"Sure," he answered with a slight nod. Ashley was aware that Mason stood close behind her and she noted Matt's gaze lifted to his friend's face. "I guess you get to drop Tyler off later?" he asked with a triumphant grin.

She turned to Mason. A light ruddiness had spread up to his cheeks, or maybe he was just flushed from the dances they'd shared. "I can give you a lift," he said quietly. It wasn't just a statement; it was a request, an offer, a hope.

"Thanks for the dances," she replied as a shy smile lit her face. "I had fun, but I want to get home and Matt's going now, so I'll just ride with him. You stay and enjoy yourself," she said. Turning again to leave, she nearly collided with Matt, who had silently stepped close. He let her slip past, and then with a hand to the small of her back, filled the space behind her as he guided her toward the exit.

They rode in silence back to the great Victorian home where Ashley's apartment was located. She'd texted Allison and Shelby to let them know where she had gone and received a "wink" icon from one and a "You go, girl" from the other in response. Friends! When Matt pulled into the drive and parked the late 1960's model Corvette, he cut the engine and hurried to open the door for her.

As they strode to the entrance of her apartment, Ashley noted, "You seem extra quiet tonight?"

"Extra quiet?" he echoed as he drew his eyebrows down in concentration. "I didn't realize we knew each other well enough that you'd know what my norms are," he said quietly.

Ashley was aware that they hadn't known each other long. Not long at all. But she also felt a soul-deep certainty that she did know him and had formed a strange connection to him. She couldn't explain it – didn't want to examine it. She surely didn't want to explore it. But she knew it was there.

The wind whipped loose snow around them, pulling the crystals from the roof and sprinkling them over the pair as they stood facing each other. His blond curls danced in the breeze as he regarded her. Gazing up into Matt's face, watching as the hard shadows played across his features, Ashley had a flash of another image. Like a photo that she'd meant to capture, she saw it clearly in her mind – in her memory.

Ashley closed her eyes tightly as her mind gave her a glimpse of the night she'd fallen and hit her head. She'd crashed to the hard concrete patio and smacking her head against the wall as she'd careened out of control. When she had opened her eyes, this man had been kneeling at her side regarding her intently. The lights from the windows had battled with the shadows of the night, and she had reached for her camera then to capture the effect.

"Are you okay?" his voice was laced with worry as it registered. Past or present, she wasn't sure, but the sound was soothing. "Ashley. Are you okay?" he asked again with growing concern. And then his hands closed around her shoulders. She felt his strength through her winter coat and leaned toward him, but still didn't answer. He pulled her close, tucking her into the crook of his arm and simultaneously taking the key from her gloved hand. "Come on," said with authority, "I'm getting you inside."

He'd guided her into the apartment, helped her out of her coat and settled her on the couch as he'd wrapped her in a blanket. She knew it wasn't fair, but she still hadn't answered whether she was alright or not. Since she wasn't certain herself, how could she tell him? Now she watched as he brought a cup of tea to her and settled next to her on the couch.

"Here, if this doesn't help, I'm taking you back to the ER," he threatened with a smile.

"Thanks, Matt," she said as she looked up into his bright blue eyes. "I don't think it will come to that. I think …"

"What?"

"I think I just had a shimmer of a memory from the night I fell," she said uncertainly. "You were kneeling beside me … my head hurt like a … and my arm and my … well, where I landed," a self-conscious laugh escaped from her lips as she spoke. "And you were there … the light dancing on the contours of your face …" her fingers lightly touched his forehead, traced his brow, trailed across his cheek, and then followed the planes to his lips before he pulled back. She continued to speak as though in a trance, "The passions played in your eyes. You were hurt, and angry, but you still could show such compassion and caring for me," she said before falling silent.

Matt's heartbeat raced as she'd laid a gentle hand to his face. But now it felt as though his heart had stopped cold: Ashley's memory was back. Would this change her mind about staying in a small town? Would she leave Miller's Bend? Everyone always left. He surged to his feet and backed away. "That's great. I'm glad for you," he said, trying to convince her – trying to convince himself. "What happens now?" he added as he tried to focus on anything but the feelings she had started churning within him.

She watched Matt's retreat a moment. Confusion and disappointment replaced the wistful look of wonder Ashley had borne as she had spoken of the night she fell. "No, Matt," she answered. "I'm not ready. It was just a picture in my mind – without context. This was a millisecond out of missing weeks." She dropped her gaze to her hands which clutched at the blanket in which she was wrapped. "It's not enough … I don't have my memory back."

Emotions swirled through Matt as he watched her. Joy swept through him when Ashley declared that she wasn't ready to leave. The feeling was followed, of course, by guilt for being happy that she wasn't healed. He felt sad for her because she'd lost a part of herself with her memory; he felt sad for himself because he was certain he would lose part of himself if she decided to leave.

She'd come to stand before him, wrapped in the blanket that trailed behind her like a robe worn by royalty. She'd glided to him while he'd been immobilized by his feelings and now she gazed at him with curiosity and caring. "What's the matter?" she asked quietly. "Did I get it wrong? Is it a dream instead of a memory?"

"No," he said gruffly. "You got it right. Your memories are in there," he whispered, as he tapped a finger lightly to her temple. "They're coming." *And then you'll go.* He started to turn away from her to regain some distance.

"Why does that bother you?" she asked. Her brows drew together in concentration and she laid a hand to his arm to stop his retreat. "Is there something about that night you don't want me to remember?"

"What?" he breathed out the question. "No. There's no reason to hide anything from that night."

"Nobody ever talks about it," she reflected. "Even Allison and Andrew haven't said anything about the wedding since they've been back."

"If we talk about it, you won't realize when your memories come," he said. "You won't know if you are remembering or if you are imagining the scenes you've heard described."

"Maybe. But I didn't imagine you kneeling over me. I have feelings that go with my shimmer of a memory," she explained, speaking so softly that he moved closer to her again. "Strong feelings."

The impact of his words caught up with Ashley. It sounded as though someone had organized the idea that no one would talk about the night of the fall. Had Matt put that much thought into her recovery?

She stepped close – too close – and then wrapped her arms around his waist and leaned against his chest. He hesitated and then almost against his will, Matt's arms enveloped her and held her gently. Definitely against his better judgment.

After several minutes, she shifted in his arms, tipped her head and peered into his face. An impulse to kiss her swept through Matt, but he pushed it aside. In its wake was the knowledge that he wanted more than a kiss – more than a hundred kisses. He yearned to know her spirit and her mind; he wanted to help her regain her memory; he wanted to help her heal.

Her lips brushed his cheek before she stepped back. "Thanks for taking care of me again," she said in a low voice.

"No problem. Damsels in distress are my thing," he said with a strangled laugh. Moving subtly away from her toward the exit, he added, "Always on call." And then more seriously he asked, "You'll be okay?"

"Yeah. I'll be okay," she confirmed.

Instinctively he knew the only way to protect himself – protect his heart – was to leave the apartment. Leave her alone and stop seeking her out. He liked her and felt a connection to her, but he knew deep in his heart, that if he let himself care for Ashley any more than he already did, it would destroy him if she decided to leave town.

CHAPTER EIGHT

"I just don't understand what's happening around here," Catherine lamented as she and the staff of the Chronicle stared at the current issue of the newspaper which lay on the mailing table. "How could this have happened?"

Tim, the young graphic artist, and Bobbie, the veteran on the staff, both shook their heads in disbelief. "This is the worst yet," Bobbie said. "I mean … some of the things that have happened were probably honest mistakes and typos, but this …" she let her voice trail off as she gestured toward the copy of the newspaper.

"This had to be intentional," Tim added with disgust. "But, who would do this?" The young man's gaze traveled from the error-riddled front page to Catherine, Charlie, and Bobbie before coming to rest on Ashley. "It seems to be a new development. Let's see … what's changed recently? Oh, yeah … there's the new girl." He said in mock surprise. "Could there be a correlation?"

Ashley felt her cheeks burn at the insinuation, but didn't respond. The front page was a garbled mess. The staff had worked hard to put out the weekly edition and it had gone to press Friday evening. When she arrived at the office this morning, she found the staff in an uproar because the stories had been changed … the headlines were on the wrong stories, typos riddled the writing, and photographs didn't match up with cutlines. And worst of all, the stories with her byline had random words thrown in, paragraphs rearranged and made no sense. If the copies had been mailed out, she and the whole staff would have looked incompetent in the eyes of the community.

"Of course not," Catherine declared in Ashley's defense. "We can't blame this on poor Ashley. But someone is trying to do us dirt!"

"We'll figure it out later," Charlie said in his quiet way. "Right now, we need to reset everything on the front page, see if there are mistakes inside and fix them, and then get it back to the printer. We have to re-print the whole batch. The mailing will be a day late, but it's the best we can do."

"The stories should be right in the computers," Ashley pointed out. "We just need to print them and go from there. We shouldn't need to reset them, should we?"

Charlie nodded, causing his gray-haired comb-over to slip forward. He pushed it back as he walked toward the paste-up area. "You're right. We'll just need to wax them and get them onto a new layout page." He flipped the switches on the printers and the waxer as he passed the machines. "Ashley, start Neal's computer and get his stories, would you please?"

The others moved to their work stations and Ashley pulled her own laptop from her bag, placed it on her desk and hit the power button. It didn't matter whether she got her own stories reprinted from her computer first or if she got Neal's. She moved to his desktop computer and powered it up. As she waited, she called to Charlie, "Where is Neal anyhow?"

"He doesn't work on Mondays," he answered. "Besides, it'll be faster without him."

Ashley's quick intake of breath caught Charlie's attention. "What?" he demanded kindly.

"Umm … I think you better look at this," she replied quietly. Ashley didn't believe in making accusations, but this was damning evidence. Charlie had moved around behind her and was looking blankly at the computer monitor. She glanced up and saw the questions in Charlie's aged face and realized that he didn't know what to look for. "See this icon?" she asked as she tapped the image of a folder on the computer screen. Then she double-clicked on it and it opened as she continued, "It's called 'special edition'."

"So?"

"So, the documents inside are garbled copies of my stories," she explained. "The replacement stories … the *wrong* stories … that *accidently* got printed … They are saved on Neal's computer."

Charlie let out a string of words that was his version of swearing, but wouldn't have gotten a kindergartener placed into time out. "That no-good snake in the grass," he concluded. "That's it! He's done!" Charlie's anger was quick to come and quick to pass. Ashley watched the others' reactions for a clue as to what had happened – who had done this and why? Neal was the obvious choice, given that he'd stated outright that he intended to get the newspaper away from Catherine. But was he really the saboteur? She would visit with Catherine and Charlie about the possibilities later … after the replacement issue was printed and mailed.

That afternoon, after the flurry of activity necessary to get the issue reprinted, Ashley sat in Catherine's office with the old couple. While Catherine was frustrated about the attempt to damage the newspaper's reputation, she wasn't devastated or consumed by it. "It was probably just a fluke with the computers," she said philosophically. "You can't trust them, you know."

"It's not the computers that we can't trust," Charlie retorted sharply. "We've got a traitor in our ranks." A former United States Navy man who had served in World War II, Charlie was not inclined to overlook traitorous activity … and sabotage in the workplace fell into that category. Turning his attention to Ashley, he asked, "Isn't there any way to tell who used Neal's computer last night?"

"Not really. You don't have the computers password protected, so anyone can use them. There might have been fingerprints, but I would have messed them up when I started it up today," Ashley answered. "I think you have to look at motive. Who would benefit from making you look bad?"

"Why would anyone want to do that?" Catherine asked as she straightened her spine. "My family has run this paper for more than 100 years. There was some nastiness decades ago, when there were two newspapers in town. But not now."

"What about the Shopper?" Ashley inquired, referring to the tabloid advertising publication also based in Miller's Bend. "Isn't there competition between you and them?"

Catherine's snort and expression showed mild contempt. "They are no competition. This is a newspaper and they are just a shopper. Not the same thing at all."

"I think it had to be one of your staff members. Is anyone unhappy about the way you run things?" Ashley asked. "Or … what about the company that does your printing? Someone there had to have known the pages got switched! Is there any reason they would want to hurt you?"

"Let's just forget about this," Catherine commanded. "Did I ever tell you about the history of this building?" The old woman's eyes twinkled as she geared up to tell a story that Ashley could tell she cared deeply about.

"No. What about the building?" Ashley asked with rising curiosity.

"It's got quite a history," Charlie interjected, before gesturing to his wife and partner. "Catherine loves to tell people about it. You'll have to learn it so you can keep the heritage alive after we move on."

Confusion rippled through Ashley as she took in the statement. Why would she have to learn the story? "What do you mean?" she inquired, her gaze resting on Charlie. He was looking tired, even for a man in his upper 80s. The labor and stress of owning and operating a business seemed to wear heavily on him some days, but other days he was full of energy and optimism.

Catherine patted Ashley's hand, drawing her attention. "Never mind that for today. Do you want to hear the story?" Catherine took a sip from her ever-present Styrofoam coffee cup and grimaced. "Awk! It's cold," she sputtered as she set the cup aside. Ashley's cell phone buzzed in her pocket and noted an incoming call from Shelby. She pushed the "ignore" button and slipped the phone back into her pocket. When she glanced up, Catherine was watching her intently. "You're not going to answer it?"

Ashley shook her head slightly as she replied, "She'll leave a message."

"Seems rude to me … not answering a call. What if it's important?" Catherine quizzed.

"Everybody leaves voice mails, they don't consider it rude if you don't answer," Ashley explained. "I could be interviewing someone, or talking with a customer … or with my boss. Shelby will understand."

"Humph."

"The building?" Ashley prompted gently. "You were going to tell me about the history?"

"Oh, yes," Catherine responded. "Did you know this is the oldest brick building in the county?"

Ashley responded by shaking her head in a negative response. The tale was underway, and Catherine was in her glory as she expounded on the long and interesting history of the building and the Chronicle. When she returned to her desk, Ashley knew that the building was constructed prior to 1880 at the south end of Main Street. It originally housed a bank, as did three other buildings in town. The newspaper also was founded in 1880, but its offices were in the basement of a building that now housed a retail store at the north end of Main Street. In those days, the newspaper was published weekly in the office, prepared for mailing and then transported by strong men using handcarts, to the train depot, where it was loaded in a cargo railcar. The arrival and departure of the train dictated the production time of the newspaper. "If we missed the train, the news didn't go out," Catherine had explained. "Sometimes we would bribe the railway officials to delay the train if we were running behind," she added with a laugh. "The scoundrels would always take the money, but they wouldn't always hold the train."

The Chronicle had begun as one of five newspapers in the county, and as hard times hit, one by one, the others had fallen away, until only the Chronicle remained. "The last competitor was closed up in 1991," Catherine lamented. "We were friends with the publishers for two generations and they tried to sell the paper to us the night before they announced that the Observer would cease to exist."

The story of the oldest brick building in the county didn't merge with the story of the Chronicle until the 1940s. A drifter with a questionable past had shown up in the trading center that later became Miller's Bend. He originally founded the newspaper and operated the business, collecting news and selling advertising for a paper that averaged four pages each week. When investigators from out East showed up asking questions, the drifter disappeared without a backward glance, Catherine related to Ashley. Another man took over as publisher for about a decade, but he lost the business in a poker game. The winner tried to run it, but didn't have any clue what he was doing. "Looking at the back copies," Catherine confided in a conspiratorial tone, "I'm not sure he could read, much less write."

"The town's elders persuaded my father to run the paper until someone suitable could be found," she explained. With a laugh, she added, "That was in 1911. It's been in my family ever since." Ashley learned that Catherine's father served as the publisher and editor until his death in 1953, at which time Catherine's mother had taken the helm. Catherine, who had worked in several newspapers in Minnesota, and held a public relations position in Washington, DC, returned home to Miller's Bend to take over when her mother's health began to fail.

The building, on the other hand, had been built as a bank and sported two rooms that were built-in vaults, complete with locks that required a combination to be dialed in to open them. The bank flourished until the 1930s and the depression overtook the country. Several banks failed, including the one housed in the building that would later become the Chronicle.

After sitting empty for a number of years, the building was converted into a mercantile on the main floor with offices in the second story, accessible by an outside stairway.

Catherine's father had purchased the building when the owner was convicted of running a house of ill repute in the upstairs "offices". It was her father who moved the newspaper office into the historic building. Catherine had invested in refurbishing the building and taken the steps necessary to have it placed on the National Register of Historic Places.

As Ashley mulled over all that she'd learned, the office phone rang and the call was transferred to Ashley's desk. When she answered, Shelby excitedly announced in her ear, "Why aren't you home yet? I left you a message more than an hour ago!"

"Sorry, I haven't checked my messages. I was visiting with Catherine and Charlie," Ashley explained. "What's up?"

"Since you didn't come on your own, I'm picking you up," Shelby declared through the phone. "I'm waiting outside."

Ashley had closed her laptop and slipped it into her bag as she listened. Now she slipped into her coat, grabbed her bag and headed for Shelby's minivan. Once inside, she demanded, "What on earth is going on?"

Her long-time friend slid a sly glance her way and answered with a pert, "You'll see."

The drive was brief and they arrived at Mrs. Holmes' house - Ashley's apartment - just as a uniformed man was latching the tailgate on a semi-trailer. Shelby parked the van and the man approached quickly. "This the owner?" he asked in a gravelly voice as he peered inside the minivan.

"Yep," Shelby confirmed with a nod of her head that sent her blond curls bouncing. "That she is."

"Good." The man handed a clipboard through the open window. "Sign on the 'x's, and I can get back on the road."

Ashley refused to accept the clipboard. She waived her hand in a gesture telling Shelby to pass it back to the man. "I don't sign anything I haven't read," she said as she hurriedly pushed the passenger side door open and surged to her feet. Nauseating dizziness made the world around her swirl and dark blotches polluted her field of vision. Sinking to her knees on the snow-covered street, she waited for the symptoms to pass.

She pinched her eyes closed and prayed for her world to get back to normal. *Why do I have to be so weak?* She finished the thought with the consolation that at least the only people to witness her episode were Shelby, who loved her, and the truck driver, whom she would never see again. Suddenly Ashley was wrapped in the warmth of a hug, and she leaned into it, grateful for the support of her good friend. Drawing in a deep fortifying breath, she realized that the scent was a man's cologne, not Shelby's perfume and she tried to pull away.

"Just hold still until it passes," a deep, rich voice advised close to her ear.

"Matt?" Her voice was barely more than a whisper and overflowing with relief. "How did you get here?"

She felt the rumble of a laugh as he answered, "I drove."

"I meant *why* are you here?" she clarified as she tentatively pulled her right eye open and peeked shyly at him. He balanced on the balls of his feet and pulled Ashley gently up with him as he rose. "Riley called me to help unload the truck," he said matter-of-factly. "Feeling better?" Matt asked quickly as he scanned her face and she nodded slightly. The action prompted an increase in the queasiness and she closed her eyes again. "You look pale – let's get you inside."

Still holding Ashley close, Matt started for the apartment door. He wondered if it was normal for her to continue to suffer from dizziness and other symptoms this long since the injury, but he could wait until later to find out. “Do you want some water, or maybe tea? Is there some medicine you should take?” he prompted as they moved forward.

The truck driver with the clipboard appeared in front of the pair, blocking their path to the entrance. “Hey lady, I’m sorry you’re feeling under the weather, but I need to have signatures,” the man implored. “I hope you’re feeling better soon, but I can’t wait. I have another delivery about three hours away.” He glanced meaningfully at his watch. “I should have been twenty miles down the road by now.”

Still bracing against Matt’s support, Ashley reached for the clipboard. “Fine,” she muttered as she signed by the first ‘x’. Shelby, carrying Jacob on her hip, appeared next to Ashley. Ashley noted the fact and assumed that Riley must have taken Isabelle and gone inside. The driver flipped the page and she signed the second spot. When he flipped to the third page, she asked, “What did you deliver anyway?” She scrawled her name on the final document.

The answer came, accompanied by a giggle, from Shelby. “The entire contents of your apartment back East,” she said.

“My apartment?” Ashley echoed as if the words made no sense.

“Yes,” her friend replied. “Come on in and you’ll see.” Shelby moved carefully down the steps to the basement apartment, still carrying Jacob. Matt released Ashley and followed closely as she descended the steps. She noted the row of boxes that lined the wall in the hallway before entering the living room. Riley who had, as Ashley suspected, taken Isabelle and stripped her out of her coat, hat and mittens, took Jacob from Shelby and began the same process with his son.

Ashley was stunned to see that there were more boxes in the living room. "This can't be everything," she finally said as her brow furled in confusion. "I should have had furniture too, not just boxes."

Shelby was busying herself in the kitchen, preparing hot drinks for everyone. Before she could pop her head around the corner to answer, Riley replied, "That's all in a shed at my parents' place."

Ashley's disorientation was growing. She felt like everyone knew what was going on but her. Tears welled in her eyes as the frustration of her accident and memory loss rolled together with the irritation of feeling completely out of control. Shelby reappeared from the kitchen bearing a tray laden with hot drinks – another favor that Ashley hadn't asked for. And then she realized that Matt had stayed close by her side, and at seeing her rising agitation, he'd begun to gently rub her shoulder. It was soothing and at the same time annoying. Annoying that he would assume she wanted to be soothed. Her voice quavered slightly as she stepped away from Matt, glanced between her friends, and said, "Could someone please tell me – from the beginning – what is happening here?"

Riley shot a quick look at his wife. "You didn't tell her? No wonder she's so … well …. upset."

"Didn't exactly get a chance to tell her -" Shelby began, but then switched her focus to Ashley. "Sorry. But if you had listened to your voicemail, you'd know …"

"Know what?" Ashley demanded, still battling the bewilderment.

"Good news," Shelby chimed in a falsely cheery voice. "You don't have to go back East. Apparently you made arrangements to have your apartment packed up and delivered to our house." She slipped a mug of steaming chamomile tea into Ashley's hand. "Here. Drink this," she added.

The mug was too hot to hold and Ashley wasn't interested in drinking right now. She quickly set the mug back on the tray Shelby had taken it from. "You learned of this … when?" she quizzed her friend.

"When the truck driver rang the doorbell this afternoon," Shelby retorted. "Riley was still home on his lunch break and the kids were a mess," she paused and perched her hands on her hips. "It wasn't very convenient at all."

"I imagine not!"

"So I called your cell phone *right away*," Shelby continued. "Did you return my call? No … that would have been too easy."

"I was at work!"

"So that means you can't return a call from your *best friend?*" Shelby's voice had risen sharply. "I was trying to help you!" She turned away as tears formed in her eyes.

"Hey ladies," Riley said in a quiet tone as he moved to hold his wife. "Let's take it down a notch here."

Ashley turned away at the same time and was surprised to find Matt had stayed close to her. His expression was uncertain, but she accepted his silent invitation for a hug as well. The toddlers played on a blanket on the floor, and all was quiet for a moment while the women regained their composure.

Both women apologized and when everyone had taken a seat, Riley told the rest of the story. The truck driver had been in a hurry and they couldn't reach Ashley. Riley had checked with his parents to see if they could unload the truck into a shed on the farm. He'd picked up Matt to help with the lifting and carrying. Shelby had come up with the idea that the boxes should go to Ashley's apartment. When they were nearly done unloading, and Ashley's signature would be needed, Shelby had gone to pick her up.

"So everything I own is either here or at your parents' place?" Ashley asked Riley.

He nodded in confirmation. "As far as we know, that's right."

Ashley covered her face. "I feel so foolish," she said quietly. "You've done so much for me and I acted like a complete loon."

Shelby hugged her friend close. "It's okay, Ash. I've known you a long time and you *are* a loon," she said with sisterly love. "You're entitled to snap once in a while."

"No, I should have let you explain," Ashley replied. Her gaze traveled from box to box and she let out a long sigh. "Looks like I've got some unpacking to do. Maybe I'll find something to explain why I quit my job. And why I had all my belongings shipped to you."

Hours later Ashley stared at the documents she'd found. Her hand shook a little as she dialed Shelby's number and waited. It went to voicemail and Ashley tried to sound normal as she left a message, "Hey Shelby. This is Ashley. I think I need a lawyer. Call me back."

She placed the phone on the coffee table and began to pace again. Stopping in front of the mirror, Ashley looked herself in the eye and asked in all seriousness, "What did you do?"

CHAPTER NINE

Ashley watched the lawyer carefully as he scanned the documents she'd taken to their meeting. Shelby and Riley had both recommended she see Mason Alexander for her legal advice. Shelby assured Ashley that he had established himself as a "good guy" and an excellent lawyer.

She'd been able to get an appointment with him first thing Tuesday morning and had let Catherine know she would be late arriving at the office. Of course, if Ashley was correctly interpreting the papers she had found, there would be no reason for Catherine to object to her tardiness.

He grimaced slightly at something he saw on one of the documents and Ashley held her breath. "Is it bad?" she asked with anxiety lacing her voice.

Mason raised his gaze to meet the client's. Absently she noted his dark brown eyes and blond hair would have been attractive to her before … that was the combination she had always thought handsome. But suddenly, she was picturing Matt. It wasn't his eye or hair color that made him attractive – it was his caring and attentiveness, his need to help others.

Mason responded with a quiet, “Not at all,” and resumed perusing the documents.

An uncharacteristic awkwardness descended on Ashley as she looked at Mason. They had danced Friday night, and she had known that he was unhappy about letting her get a ride home with Matt. Was he still bothered by it? Should she bring it up? “I didn’t realize you were a lawyer the other night …”

He glanced up from the papers again with a hint of amusement. “Would that have made a difference?” he asked with a smile. And then with a shake of his head, he added, “Just kidding. Don’t worry about it.” He looked back to the papers in his hand.

Ashley tried looking around the room as she waited. But the office was decorated in a no-nonsense, utilitarian style, and soon her gaze returned to rest on the man seated behind the heavy mahogany desk. He was well muscled for a person whose profession kept him in an office, and she noted he had a rich tan that was out of place in mid-winter on the northern plains. “Do you travel a lot?” she blurted.

Mason laid the papers on his desk and turned his attention to Ashley. “More than most people around here, I suppose,” he replied.

“They don’t really get out of town too often, do they?” she agreed with a smile.

“You’ve traveled?” Mason queried.

Nodding, Ashley answered, “For work. I’ve been to dozens of countries and all over the United States.”

“What made you want to buy a business in Miller’s Bend?” Mason asked. “Surely with your background you would have found some other place to settle down? Perhaps someplace more exciting?” His dark eyes studied her steadily as he waited for her to form her reply. Mason wasn’t certain why her answer mattered, but he sincerely hoped that she honestly wanted to stay in Miller's Bend; he hoped that she wasn't out to turn a fast dollar, while somehow exploiting the ancient couple who had operated the community newspaper for generations.

"I …" Ashley stalled as she wondered how much to share with the lawyer. She'd been flabbergasted when she discovered the documents and wanted a professional to confirm that she was interpreting them correctly. Rather than answer – either fully or partially – she responded with a question of her own. Once again she asked for confirmation, "So you mean I really did purchase the business here in Miller's Bend? I am reading the papers correctly?"

Mason had returned the documents to the folder she had presented them in. "Yes, Miss Nelson. According to what I've seen here," he said as he tapped the folder and then slid it toward Ashley, "you are the sole proprietor of The Chronicle." He paused, bestowing an endearing smile on her and added, "… and the county's oldest brick building." He stood and walked slowly around the desk, almost as if sneaking up on a skittish animal, until he stood near Ashley before he cleared his throat. "How is it that you were not aware that you purchased The Chronicle?" He waited a moment, hoping for a reasonable, *believable* answer.

"I …," again, she stopped. With downcast eyes, she answered softly, "I don't remember." When Mason didn't respond, she cautiously looked up to check his expression. He leaned casually against the desk, but radiated confidence and something else. Suspicion.

"You don't remember an entire lifestyle change?" he asked skeptically. With eyebrows raised, he regarded Ashley quietly a moment before continuing, "You quit your job, bought a business and moved to a new community … and you don't remember any of it?"

"I've got a little case of amnesia -" she began

"Amnesia is extremely rare, as I understand it," he interrupted her explanation.

The need to defend herself had Ashley on the verge of telling him to call the hospital and check her story, but she held her tongue. She rose instead and reached for the folder. "You said everything was in order, right? The whole transaction was completed?"

Mason moved aside and handed the folder to Ashley as he let out a deep sigh. "Look, Miss Nelson," he said, "I hope this deal is on the up and up. If it is, I wish you all the best and look forward to doing business with you." His focus locked on Ashley's before he continued sternly, "But, there are a lot of people in this town who love and respect Catherine and Charlie. If you are trying to pull a fast one, or con them somehow, the community will rally around them and you will be running for the hills."

A stunned silence followed. Ashley felt the flush of irritation at the man's bold words. "I assure you that is not the case." Her words were crisp and clear, direct and honest.

Ashley had risen, buttoned her winter coat, slid the folder with the documents into her bag and shouldered it. She stepped toward the door, and when Mason said nothing further, she turned to face him again. Before she formed a thank you, he uncrossed his arms, which he had held stubbornly across his chest, and took a step toward her.

"How can you be so sure? What with your amnesia and all?" he asked with a hint of a taunt in his voice. "You don't remember anything."

"I remember who I am," she answered vehemently. "I am not a person who would con anyone. A assure you, I don't operate that way."

"But your amnesia … You said yourself that you don't remember anything about this purchase," he pressed.

Ashley faced Mason squarely. "The amnesia only affects a few weeks preceding my latest concussion which I suffered when I fell recently." She took a steadying breath. "Memories from longer ago are intact." She turned and pulled open the door. Ashley paused, glanced back over her shoulder and said, "Thank you for your professional advice. I appreciate your time."

The bitter taste of indignation hung in the back of Ashley's throat as she made her way toward the Chronicle. How dare the man accuse her of trying to con Catherine and Charlie? To the outside world she was simply an employee of the Chronicle, but now that Ashley was certain that she had interpreted the documents correctly, she was growing increasingly more excited about the prospect – no, the reality – of owning the business. Her mind raced ahead, thinking of changes, improvements she could make. She would bring the weekly newspaper into the 21st century.

Her determined steps faltered as she passed in front of the bank. She shouldn't carry the documents around with her. Ashley quickly changed course, entering the bank and greeting the receptionist. "I need to rent a safe deposit box," she announce breathlessly. As an afterthought she added, "I suppose I should open an account, as well."

The woman smiled pleasantly and led her to the office of a personal banker who took care of the necessary paperwork. When that was completed, Ashley was escorted to the vault that housed the safe deposit boxes, and shown her box, which was opened for her. She was left alone to slip her valuables into the box. Ashley smiled as she put the box back in its space, closed the door and twisted the key to lock it. The proof that she'd purchased the business was locked away.

Bidding the receptionist a good day, Ashley stepped out into the mid-morning sunshine and smiled. She felt as though she had come through the darkest period and things were beginning to fall into place. Casting her eyes skyward, she breathed a quiet, "Thank you, God," before continuing down the street toward her job. *No*, a voice in her head corrected. *It's more than that; it's your future.*

As she approached the building – the oldest brick building in the county – Ashley's smile broadened. Maybe the past didn't matter so much, now that she had a plan – an embryo of a plan – for what lay ahead. The feeling of being out of control, helplessly tossed around in the abyss of the unknown, was abating; the feelings of authority and direction were growing steadily.

The Chronicle, as well as the building that housed it, and the responsibility to maintain its integrity were hers and the sense of pride that washed over her was almost overwhelming. All the work she'd done for corporations in the past years didn't mean anything to her in comparison. She now had ownership, responsibility and a whole lot of work to do. She would lead the staff in transitioning the production from printing out the stories, cutting and waxing them, placing them physically on layout sheets and driving them to the printing plant, to the new technology of computer generated editions. They would design the pages within the computers and send them electronically to the printer. She would set up a web presence and use social media to promote the newspaper. For the first time in a long time, Ashley felt excitement and anticipation.

She pushed the door open and stepped into the front office, eager to talk with Catherine and Charlie about the transition. The smile died on her lips as she looked around. Soot covered the counter top, walls, desks, tables, computers, paste-up banks and, well, pretty much every surface. The staff members wore their coats and looked miserable. "What happened?" she asked with astonishment. "What's going on?"

"Not that you'd really care, since you're temporary," Neal began, "but there's a bit of trouble with the furnace." He pointed to the steps which lead to the basement. "They're working on it now."

"What kind of trouble?"

He had quickly powered down his computer and shrugged as he raised his face to look at Ashley. "Don't know. Don't care," he said as he rose and slid into his coat. "Now that you're here, I can head out for my interview."

Ashley's instinct from the first time she'd met the man had been one of distrust. It seemed that he was forever "heading out" for one thing or another, but rarely produced much news copy. Worse yet, as Ashley got acquainted with people around town, she was hearing complaints about Neal's writing. Apparently, his personality rubbed people the wrong way and irritated many, but he also seemed to have developed the habit of misquoting people and blowing things out of proportion in his news coverage. Neal's behavior was one of the things she would have to address as the new owner of the Chronicle.

As Ashley pondered Neal's behavior, a repair man emerged from the basement where he'd been working on the furnace. He barely seemed to notice Ashley as he passed her and headed to the back office. A minute later, Catherine buzzed Ashley's phone and asked her to come to her office.

"Good morning, Catherine," she greeted her mentor. "Sorry I wasn't here sooner."

Catherine waved off the apology. "You're here now. This young man is about to give us the verdict on the furnace," she said as she swung her gaze toward the heating and cooling technician. Ashley gauged him to be nearing 60 years of age, but all things being relative, that would make him a "young man" in Catherine's view.

"We can set up something temporary," the man, whose uniform indicated his name to be Brent, said. "But that furnace has breathed its last. You have to replace it." He paused and glanced nervously around.

"Ashley," Catherine said, "what would you suggest we do?" The old woman watched Ashley steadily as she waited for the response.

"Well … I'd say we need to get the temporary heat operational, get a cleaning crew in here and then ask the heating and cooling businesses in town for bids on a new heating system," she replied confidently.

Catherine nodded in agreement and gave a quick smile in response. She turned her gaze on the repair man as she ordered, "That's what I'd do, too. You'd better get busy. We need heat and we need to get back to work."

"There's more," Brent began in a normal voice. He glanced meaningfully at Ashley and she had the feeling that she was supposed to disappear. He waited. She waited.

It was Catherine, whose lack of patience was infamous around the community, who broke the silence. "Well? What is it?" she nearly barked the question.

"I don't know if you want the whole staff to know this …" he replied. He still glared at Ashley as if trying to banish her.

"Oh, she's fine," Catherine replied as she waved a hand dismissively. "In fact, Ashley is working closely with Charlie and me these days."

Brent's shocked silence was not a good indicator of how the news was going to be received around the community. Ashley thought he'd been glaring before, but now his expression darkened. Finally he spoke. "I'd recommend you call the police, Ma'am. It is my opinion that the furnace was vandalized." With that he turned and strode away.

Ashley was dismayed when, within minutes of calling the police department to report Brent's assessment, Police Chief Schuster and an officer who was introduced as Josh Pendleton, as well as the county sheriff, Erik Dunn, all had converged in the newspaper office. *Only in a small town,* she thought. Ashley mostly stayed out of the way and listened as Catherine repeated Repairman Brent's assertion that the furnace had been vandalized. Pendleton hastily headed to the basement to confer with Brent about the damage and to document it.

"Have there been any other incidents? Suspicious events?" Schuster asked of Catherine.

Ashley remembered the middle-aged chief of police from the days following her fall, when he had repeatedly visited her to be sure she didn't need anything. Even after he determined that the incident had indeed been an accident and not an assault, he continued to check on her until she was released from the hospital. When he had questioned her, it felt more like visiting with her uncle than a police inquiry. She was impressed by his kind, friendly approach to police work.

"Yes," Charlie confirmed with sadness tainting his response. "Yes, there have been."

Catherine, who hadn't answered, shot a quick look at the man she'd spent more than 50 years with – in business and in her home. Her features softened as she gazed at Charlie. "Yes," she confirmed in a reserved voice.

The chief pulled up a chair and sat, glancing expectantly between the two, waiting for one or the other to break loose with the story of what had been going on inside the walls of the oldest brick building in the county. "Well?" Schuster prodded.

Sheriff Dunn sighed heavily, leaned against the doorjamb and checked his watch. He'd been hoping to receive word today about the missing woman, Chrissi – the one Matt Vander Meer and Mason Alexander had set him on the trail of days before. Detectives in Chicago were investigating the information Matt's stepfather had provided and he'd passed on to them. Now all he could do was wait for their call.

Charlie's voice brought Dunn back to the present issue. The questions about Chrissi would have to wait until later. Dunn, with pen poised over his notepad, waited as Charlie began to recount some of the occurrences that had come to pass recently at the Chronicle.

He explained about the edition that had been printed with the stories in disarray, and that it had had to be reprinted, delaying the delivery of the newspaper, and causing considerable additional expense. Charlie's anger edged through his normally calm persona. "I just can't believe one of our staff would do this – but it had to be someone with access to the building," he concluded. "It had to be one of us!" He choked on the last word and turned away.

"I've found the till … greatly diminished … a couple of times," Catherine confided quietly. "There's been damage to the company vehicle, too."

"Strange charges are showing up on statements from some of the stores, too," Charlie added.

Both lawmen took hurried notes as the couple talked about the things that had been happening. "Any idea who would want to make things difficult for you?" Schuster asked when they seemed to have run out of incidents to talk about. He waited as the two looked to each other for guidance.

When neither spoke, Ashley asked, "Have you had issues with Neal?"

"He's a bit on the under-motivated side," Catherine responded.

Charlie nodded in agreement. "That boy just doesn't have any fire in his belly," he added despondently. "No gumption."

Dunn, having taken more of an interest in the questioning turned to Ashley. "Why do you ask about Neal, Miss Nelson? Do you have information?"

If this had happened yesterday, she'd have stayed out of it, but now, today, she was aware that she was the owner of the Chronicle. This was her responsibility. Avoiding eye contact with either Charlie or Catherine, she spoke to the police chief and the sheriff. "He warned me the first day I started working here," she said.

"Warned you … how?" Schuster inquired.

"He said that he wanted to be sure I understood how things are … and that even though he considers himself currently to be a glorified errand boy …" she paused in her answer as she tried to remember his words. "He said he *will* be the editor. That Catherine can't hold on much longer." A stunned silence followed her statement.

The silence was broken by the persistent buzz of Dunn's cell phone. Glancing at the display, he announced that he needed to return to the office.

As Dunn rushed to the exit, Schuster turned his attention back to the trio. "Where is Neal now?" he asked. "I think I want to have a little chat with him."

Ashley replied that he'd been on his way to an interview shortly after she arrived. Catherine cut in, saying, that he was most likely camped out in the reading area of the county library.

Before Schuster headed out to find Neal and engage him in a friendly "chat", he asked for the names, contact information and work history for each of the employees.

CHAPTER TEN

Ashley pulled into the driveway of Mrs. Holmes' place and parked the aging Chevy Trailblazer. Turning the engine off, she pulled the key and dropped it into her bag, and then paused to reflect: at this time yesterday she hadn't known she owned the Chronicle, hadn't had any responsibilities other than for herself. Now she shouldered the strain, work and worry for maintaining a business and its employees, as well as the concerns of the entire community's news coverage. It was a lot to handle alone, and yet, she felt deeply thankful that she'd been given the opportunity.

Overcome with a sense of gratitude, she lowered her head and whispered, "Thank you, Lord, for bringing me to this place in my life. Please guide my steps on this new path." Ashley didn't move. She sat still in the rapidly cooling interior of the vehicle she now owned as part of the purchase of the Chronicle, reveling in appreciation for the way things had worked out.

The darkness of a late winter night enveloped the town, and although she knew that it would be best to head inside her apartment, she waited a long time before finally stepping out of the SUV. Mrs. Holmes' cheery voice rang out in the still evening, "Are you alright, dear?" As Ashley glanced up and saw the old woman framed in the doorway, with light spilling around her, she was struck with the impression that the woman seemed to glow with a welcoming aura.

"Yes, thank you," Ashley replied as she began moving toward the house. "How are you?"

"Oh, I'm fine. Do you have time to join me?" the landlord asked. She pushed the door open wider in invitation.

The tantalizing smells of a home-cooked meal met Ashley before she reached the entrance. She hadn't realized how hungry she was until she stepped inside and got the full effect of the aromas. "Can you join me for dinner?" Mrs. Holmes was saying. "I cooked way too much … It will take me all week to eat it all by myself."

Laughing, Ashley answered, "I'll do what I can to lighten your burden." She'd deposited her bag and winter coat in the chair near the entrance and followed Mrs. Holmes into the dining room of the Victorian home. Ashley's steps slowed when she saw the antique China set in a formal arrangement at three place settings.

The hostess had reached the table and turned to Ashley. "Come on … take a seat," she instructed as she indicated a chair. Ashley complied, but glanced between the two remaining place settings.

"Are you expecting another guest?"

"I had hoped that Tyler or Mathew would join us, but neither was able to," Mrs. Holmes replied with visible disappointment. "They always come if I need help, but they rarely have time just to visit or to join me for a meal. You know, just to relax and be sociable." A shadow of sadness rippled in the ghostly gray eyes of the older woman before she shook off the air of despondency. "Especially Mathew. That boy needs a distraction. Something …" Mrs. Holmes locked gazes meaningfully with Ashley before continuing, "… or *someone* fun and interesting. He needs a friend who is strong and self-sufficient, someone who doesn't need anything from him."

Ashley didn't comment, but felt warmth in her cheeks. She had found herself thinking of Matt often – too often – since her fall. Now, with Mrs. Holmes' not-too-subtle suggestion, she was thinking of him again.

A soft laugh, no doubt brought on in response to Ashley's blush, did nothing to relieve her mental discomfort. "Do you know anyone like that?" Mrs. Holmes asked gently.

Looking back into the older woman's face, Ashley smiled brightly, "Why, yes. As a matter of fact I do," she replied. And with a laugh in her voice, Ashley declared, "I believe *you* would fit the bill."

An expression of mock horror contorted the gaunt, wrinkled face of the hostess as she clutched her hands to her chest. "Touché, dear! Touché!" Then she smiled fully, with a wistful expression, and added quietly, "Oh, to be 50 years younger!"

Mrs. Holmes gave a quick prayer of thanks for the meal and the company, and for opening Ashley's heart to the new opportunities she faced. As they dined, they discussed the events since they'd spoken last. Ashley revealed her discovery that prior to her memory loss, she had purchased the Chronicle and arranged for her belongings to be shipped to Miller's Bend. Ashley explained that the transaction had been handled via phone calls and with the assistance of a broker representing Catherine and Charlie, and a lawyer representing herself. And so it was that Ashley hadn't met the newspaper pioneers until the day Shelby had sent her to the office. "Everything makes sense looking back, even if it was a bit confusing for me those first days," she concluded.

"You see, you did have a plan after all," the older woman said reassuringly. "And do you feel better – more settled – as it's becoming clear to you?"

Ashley remembered the feeling of calm and contentment that had settled over her as she waited in the car, as she thanked God for leading her here. "Yes, I do." Her reply was a quiet reflection of the humility she felt.

"When you quiet your mind, and listen for God's intentions with your heart, He will lead you to a better life," Mrs. Holmes counseled quietly. "It took a long time for me to learn that when I was young. Too long."

After a few minutes, Ashley reminded Mrs. Holmes of the conversation they'd begun a week earlier. "Do you feel like telling the rest of your story? You must have been quite a rebel."

"You really want me to tell the rest? I thought it would be boring to you," the old woman answered with a sigh. "I'm surprised you even remembered."

"Oh, I remembered," Ashley countered. "I wrote up notes after we talked last time." She met Mrs. Holmes gaze and added, "I'd like to write your story, if you'll allow it."

Mrs. Holmes' skin flushed as she waved her hand as though chasing a pesky fly and replied, "Pish-posh! No one would want to read about me. I'm just an old lady. No story there."

"I think there's a lot to you and our readers always enjoy feature stories about people they know," Ashley answered. She watched as Mrs. Holmes digested that. Ashley saw the instant that the old woman latched onto a detail in her statement.

Mrs. Holmes' gray eyes lit with mischief as she asked, "Our readers? Are you feeling some responsibility toward the community? Possessiveness about the citizens?"

"It's more than that," Ashley explained. "I would do my best, regardless of whether I had purchased the business or not.

But now I feel excited about making improvements. Also, it's very gratifying to deliver a quality newspaper."

"More gratifying than flying around the world digging up facts for someone else's story?"

Without pausing to consider her answer, Ashley confirmed Mrs. Holmes' point. "Oh, yes! Much more so."

The hostess regarded Ashley a moment longer before adding, "Of course, it has only been one day."

"Quite true," Ashley responded quietly. "I suppose I could feel completely differently tomorrow at this time."

"Oh, I believe you will enjoy the new path you've chosen," Mrs. Holmes said earnestly. "Remember that you did choose this, it wasn't thrust upon you. Always commit to the Lord whatever you do, and your plans will succeed."

They finished the meal in silence. Ashley offered to clear the table and Mrs. Holmes agreed to let her. "Normally I would put up a fuss over this treatment, but I've been extremely tired of late," she explained. When Ashley finished, the two moved to the sitting room before Mrs. Holmes began the continuation of her story.

"Do you recall what I told you?" the old woman asked. "I'm not sure where I left off …"

"I remember you were telling me about how you went out to get your college education and began your career. You also encouraged me to remember that my job doesn't define me," Ashley said. "You were right. My job is just what I do and your words helped me decide to embrace the opportunity I have in Miller's Bend, even before I discovered that I bought a business here."

A bony hand came to rest on Ashley's hand as Mrs. Holmes reached out to touch the younger woman. "That reminds me – I want to know who you've told?"

"Told?"

"That you're staying here. That you bought the Chronicle."

Confusion furrowed Ashley's brow. "Why? What does it matter? Catherine is planning to announce it in the next issue."

Shaking her head, Mrs. Holmes made a disapproving "Tsk, tsk tsk" sound, saying, "That will never do. You need to talk to Mathew. You need to tell him yourself."

"Why?" Ashley asked again. "It doesn't matter to him what I do."

"Oh, but I think it does," Mrs. Holmes countered. "He likes you, but he doesn't have much extra time or energy … what with his mother and his sister and all his responsibilities …"

Ashley's pulse was pounding loudly at the implication that Matt had an interest in her plans. Sure, he was nice, but could they be more than friends? Her voice squeaked a little as she began to protest, "We're just friends, Mrs. Holmes. I don't think it matters to him what I'm planning to do. I don't understand -"

"He likes you, but he's cautious. He doesn't have time or energy to invest in a woman who isn't staying around … one who's likely to leave," the old woman spoke fervently and grasped Ashley's hand tighter. "Don't you see? If you have a business, you'll be staying. And that might let him feel that it's safe to let his guard down and let himself care about you."

Ashley stared dumbly at the landlord. She'd thought the woman to be a sweet, kind, grandmotherly soul, but apparently she was a ruthless matchmaker as well. She'd just been biding her time before she launched the offensive. "I'm not sure he'd appreciate your help in this area," Ashley began when she'd caught her breath. "And I'm not a manipulative person -"

"Of course not! I wouldn't be trying to help you out if I thought you were," Mrs. Holmes refuted the statement. "You are a straight-shooter, and that's what he needs. He doesn't have time to play games."

"I … um … I did tell everybody Friday night at dinner that I'd decided to stay in Miller's Bend and -"

"Mathew, too?"

"Well, yes."

"And?"

"And, what?"

"How did he respond? Was he glad? Did he say anything?" Mrs. Holmes asked as she slid to the front edge of her seat. "Did you get any good vibes?"

Ashley felt the heat in her face as she recalled the way Matt's gaze had held her own. He had smiled and whispered that he was glad she was staying. Yes, he'd been happy. She nodded absently as she recalled the several encounters she'd had with him – it really did seem that he went out of his way to help her when she needed it. Maybe Mrs. Holmes was right, maybe he did like her.

"I knew it! I was sure that my Mathew likes you," the woman crowed. Then subsiding, she continued, "But you have got to tell him about the Chronicle. He has to know that you are willing to put down roots here – that you're ready to settle down."

Exasperation hit Ashley at the last comment. It was the same chorus her mother had been singing to her for the past year: settle down. "Oh, for heaven's sake, Mrs. Holmes," Ashley proclaimed. She rubbed her temples and softened her voice before continuing, "Let's just give it a rest for now, can we?"

Mrs. Holmes looked a bit chagrined as she scooted back in her chair. "Of course, dear. I guess I did get a little carried away."

"You think?"

"Well, maybe," she conceded. "It's just that I love those boys and I need to see them all settled. I'm half-way there – Riley and Andrew are alright now – there's just Mathew, and then my Tyler."

Ashley's attention had been drawn to a photo of Mrs. Holmes and a man she assumed to be the late Mr. Holmes which rested on the mantle in the sitting room. When she realized her host had quit speaking, Ashley glanced back to Mrs. Holmes' face. She wore a placid expression, with a hint of a smile and her silver eyes eerily unfocused.

Unsure whether Mrs. Holmes was imagining an unknown future or remembering a tranquil scene from the past, Ashley gently touched her again to ease the woman back to the present day. "Mrs. Holmes? Are you alright?"

Seeming to snap out of her reverie, Mrs. Holmes brought her gaze back into focus and turned her startling eyes on Ashley. She smiled with genuine warmth and replied, "Yes dear. I'm alright."

"You're certain?"

Straightening in her chair, the host replied, "Most definitely. Now … you wanted to know how I learned my lesson to listen to the Lord's will, rather than my own, when I was your age. Is that right?"

Ashley retrieved her bag which contained her laptop, notebook and pens, among other things, and returned. Settling back into her seat, she clarified, "I'm not after a particular lesson, Mrs. Holmes. You can tell me whatever parts of your story you want to. I'll just listen, and take notes."

"You'll write a story?"

"Only if it's alright with you."

Now the old woman looked to the photo displayed on the mantle. "I don't know. The story I have to tell – it is a private story. Very few people who are still alive know it … most have chosen to forget if they did know it."

A wave of anxiety flashed through Ashley's system. Did she want to know Mrs. Holmes' secrets? Was there some awful facet to the sweet woman? Beginning to put her notebook away, Ashley offered, "That's alright, Mrs. Holmes. You don't have to tell me …"

The older woman's gaze snapped back to Ashley's. "I will tell you. I intended to tell you, because it will help you personally. And in so doing, it may help Mathew. What I'm not sure, is whether I want you to write it in a story, because that is permanent. And tangible. It can be replicated."

"I would be honored if you choose to share your story with me, but please know that you don't need to," Ashley assured the older woman. "If you want me to, I could write the story and give you the only copy to do with as you wish." Ashley paused, watching for a response, before adding, "Or, if you prefer, I won't write it at all."

Mrs. Holmes nodded almost imperceptibly and, without preamble, began telling the story of so many years ago. "I didn't listen. I went away to college. It was hard because there weren't many women in college. Some of the men tried to help us, but some of the men tried to teach us a lesson. They were so hard on us to try to force us to drop out and go home where we belonged."

"It took me a very long time to realize that my aspirations had been hollow. Achieving my degree did not filled me with a sense of accomplishment," the older woman said. "I got the job I wanted in my career field. I kept trying harder and harder, but I was missing something."

"I might have appeared to have everything – independence, excitement, freedom. But what I really had was loneliness and aimlessness. The more I strived to be perfect in my professional life, the more I lost myself."

The remorse in Mrs. Holmes' voice was alarming to Ashley. How could events from several decades past have such an effect on the normally confident woman? "You seem so content now …," Ashley began in attempt to lighten the conversation. "You must have found your way to your goals eventually?"

"The goals I had set for myself were my goals, but they weren't what God had in mind for me," Mrs. Holmes said. "I refused to see it at the time, but looking back it is clear. That's why it was a struggle for me."

"It would have been a struggle for any woman at that time – trying to make it in a man's world," Ashley countered. "Like you said the other day, you were a pioneer."

"I've learned to listen for God's intentions for me. 'Commit your works to the Lord, and your thoughts will be established,'" the older woman said with conviction. "That's from Proverbs."

Ashley was enthralled by the woman's intense convictions and openness to discussion without argument. "How? How did you learn to listen?" And then, her focus dropped as she remembered several conversations with her parents in which they urged her to find a safer job – one that didn't involve traveling to exotic destinations and digging into facts that powerful people wanted left alone. They were afraid for her safety, and not without merit. She had been injured several times in the course of her work. Was it possible that the pleading of her parents was actually God speaking to her? "How do you recognize a message as truly being from Him?"

"We receive many, many messages in our lives," Mrs. Holmes spoke quietly. "Trusting your instincts is important. And I think the messages from the people who truly love us are the messages that reflect God's intentions for us. If only we can learn to listen before it's too late," she concluded.

Ashley watched Mrs. Holmes carefully. The older woman had experienced much in her lifetime, and it would be smart to learn from her experiences. "You think that your lesson came too late?" she guessed "Is that why you take in people and try to help them?"

"I didn't set out to take in renters," Mrs. Homes replied. "I never even considered it. But one day there was a person with a need of shelter … And here I was alone in this big old house … my dear sweet Harold, bless his soul, had passed away three months earlier, and I was so lonesome."

"Who was it? That first renter?"

Mrs. Holmes looked away. "You wouldn't know him. But he was a carpenter, of all things, and in exchange for staying here, he built the rooms to make the basement apartment. I encouraged Riley, Matt and Tyler to help him and they learned a lot while he was here. He eventually was able to move on, and so it began."

"You've had renters ever since?"

"Most of the time there is someone in need of a safe haven," Mrs. Holmes said with a nod and a smile. "Usually, I gain as much from their being here as they gain." The old woman's eyes were moist when her gaze met Ashley's. "God brings young people to me, and I help them out in whatever way I can," she answered. "Everyone's needs are different."

Ashley's curiosity was piqued. "What do you think you should have done instead of following your dreams back when you were younger? How would it have changed your life?"

"I can never know how my life would have gone. Some things would have changed, others would have remained untouched," she answered. "But I will tell you … there was a boy who loved me. When I left for college, he vowed to wait for me to return," Mrs. Holmes said as she focused on the past. "He said he loved me, but he didn't want to hold me back and have me feel trapped. He said, 'Go and do what you need to. I will be here when you come home. We'll start our life together then.'"

"That's so sweet," Ashley replied. "So that's him, in the photos?" she asked, indicating the framed pictures on a nearby wall. "When did you come back to Miller's Bend?"

Shadows of sadness and regret played across the older woman's face and her shoulders dropped. "No, that's not him," she said as she set her knitting aside. A tear slid down her wrinkled cheek. "I never saw him again."

"Why not?"

"Because I was foolish and arrogant," Mrs. Holmes said quietly. "I took his love for granted. I thought I could put it on a shelf and save it for later. Save it for a time that it would fit into my life and my schedule. I wasted the chance that I'd been given."

"He didn't wait for you?" Ashley surmised. Indignantly she began, "That is so typical! Men tell you they'll do this or they'll do that, but then when you turn your back … it all changes. They just go off and do what they want!"

"No. That's not what happened," Mrs. Holmes corrected sternly. "He did love me and he did wait. We wrote to each other a lot when I first left …"

"Until he became interested in someone else?"

"No. He loved me," Mrs. Holmes said with vehemence. And then more quietly, almost reverently, she repeated, "He loved me. I had endured enough pain and disappointment out there trying to pursue my dreams. I had finally decided to come home and marry him – give up my plans."

"But? What happened? Had he changed his mind?" Ashley prompted when Mrs. Holmes paused.

"No, dear. He was true, even though I hadn't been home. He loved me, but he'd been pulled up to go to Korea. He wrote to tell me, so I wouldn't waste my money traveling home only to find him gone. We decided to wait until he was back in the United States to marry and start our life together." A slight shiver rattled through the old woman as she inhaled deeply before speaking again. "He was killed in action."

"Oh. Oh, my goodness," Ashley gasped. "I'm so sorry," she said as she moved to Mrs. Holmes and hugged her lightly. "I shouldn't have said those things about him."

"I should have never left him. I should have accepted his love when I had the chance," the old woman said. "I should have listened to my heart when it told me that my plans needed to change. I lived with those pains and regrets for years."

Ashley's mind raced. Mrs. Holmes' story had to have taken place in the early 1950s. If the man in the photos wasn't her love, then who was he? The inquisitive mind of a reporter kicked into gear and she asked, "Is that when you came back to Miller's Bend?"

Mrs. Holmes' ghostly gray eyes focused on the photos briefly before she looked back to Ashley. "No. I'm afraid that's all I can give you just now. I need to rest." She stood up with grace and walked silently from the room.

Ashley silently ran through the story again in her mind. It was a great tragedy and would make for an excellent feature … maybe Mrs. Holmes would give her permission to publish it one day. A story about chances missed and fate yanking away a person's happiness. Ashley vowed that she would never allow her own chances to be taken from her.

CHAPTER ELEVEN

Traveling the world provided many benefits and one of the tidbits of wisdom Ashley had garnered from her experiences was that the village elders usually knew what they were talking about. If they shared advice with a younger member of the tribe, it should be taken to heart. The morning after visiting with Mrs. Holmes, Ashley wasn't certain how to handle much of what she'd learned, but she was certain of one thing: She needed to speak with Matt.

A quick internet search revealed that Mathew Vander Meer (age 25-30), of Miller's Bend, SD, had a studio with a landline, and more importantly, an address, which she wrote down. Ashley called, reached an answering service and left a backwards message that ended with, "If you don't call me back, I'll pick up lunch and bring it to you."

Now on her lunch break, Ashley realized that the plan was wrought with opportunity for error … but she decided to follow through and see what happened next. She was waiting in the drive-thru line at the local American-Mexican fast food place when her phone buzzed. Afraid the caller was Matt, she checked the id panel, which read MOM.

"Hi, Mom," she answered quickly.

"Are you driving?"

"No. I'm sitting in a drive-thru line," Ashley replied to sooth her mother. "It's as good as being parked."

"You left a message to call. What's up?"

Ashley's mother, Tammie, was ecstatic when Ashley shared the revelation that she had quit her job and shipped all that she owned to Miller's Bend. "Thank goodness," Tammie exclaimed. "I've been waiting for you to forget the wildness of world travel and settle down! Oh, honey, I'm so happy!"

"Settle down?" The phrase sent a sense of apprehension through Ashley. "You make it sound like I'm going to get married and have babies, Mom. Maybe take up quilting and baking."

Tammie laughed heartily at that. "Oh, no. For you 'settling down' means staying in one zip code for more than two months. This is going to be so nice. I can quit worrying about you all the time … and I can come and visit you!"

"Mom." Ashley pulled forward to the order window.

"… and you already have friends there."

"Mom." Ashley's voice was rising.

"You could get a pet … a dog would be nice," Tammie continued.

"Mom!"

"What?"

"I have to order. Just wait," Ashley said with controlled patience. She put the phone down on the seat next to her and piled a sweater over it so her mom wouldn't hear her order two meals and ask questions about that. She placed the order and pulled ahead.

"Okay, Mom," she began, when she picked up the phone again. "There's more …"

"More? *Are* you getting married?"

"Mom! No," Ashley replied in a rough voice. And then softening her tone, she explained, "I seem to have purchased a business – the local newspaper."

There was silence.

"Mom?"

"I think there's a bad connection … did you just say you bought the local newspaper?" her mother asked with an unusually calm voice. "Is that what you said?"

"Umm. Yes."

"Why? And with what?"

A horn honked nearby, giving Ashley the excuse she was desperately searching her mind for. "I have to go, Mom. I'm causing a traffic jam. Both hands on the wheel – you know. We'll talk later. Love ya – bye!" She disconnected the call and breathed deeply.

Minutes later Ashley cautiously approached a small building at the address she'd gleaned off the internet. The building didn't look like much. Prairie Wind Studio, the sign said. An image-evoking name for some sort of artist, but was this really Matt's place? She knocked on the door and waited. Ashley knocked again, and then heard noises like someone approaching the entrance. The door opened and swung wide. A solidly-built man sporting a brown uniform stepped out, nearly colliding with Ashley.

"Sorry ma'am," he said a bit abruptly. "Can I help you find something?"

The uniform registered, and combined with the name tag, she quickly remembered meeting Sheriff Erik Dunn before. He'd been at the newspaper office, although he'd seemed more concerned with something other than the sabotage at her business. He didn't seem to recognize her, and she felt a bit stung by the fact.

"Aren't you the new gal at the newspaper?" he asked. "Who are you looking for? Maybe I can head you in the right direction."

Flustered, she began to explain, "I was looking -"

"Ashley?" a deep voice asked from the doorway.

She looked up to find Matt smiling in welcome. The brightest blue eyes she'd ever encountered twinkled a bit as he asked, "You really brought me lunch?"

Feeling a blush in her cheeks, Ashley raised the bag from the fast-food restaurant and nodded. "I said I would." She paused, offered him a smile, and concluded, "Of course, I didn't know if you got my message or not."

"You said not to call you back," he reminded. "Come in." He looked to the sheriff, who wore a grin that would put the Cheshire cat to shame, and said, "Thanks, again, for the info. Keep me updated."

"Will do," Dunn replied. With a glance in the direction Ashley had taken, he added, "Keep me posted, too. And enjoy your lunch break, buddy."

Matt pushed the door closed and turned back to Ashley who was slowly, almost reverently taking in his studio. He held his breath while he waited for her reaction. The building wasn't much to look at, and once a person was inside, there was workspace and the kitchenette – no showroom. There was barely a place to sit. Normally, the table would have been cluttered with paperwork, but thankfully he had cleared it when he received the message that Ashley would be dropping by. Although he had been skeptical that she would show up. *I said*

I would, she'd reminded him at the door. Could it be that simple?

She seemed almost enchanted as she slowly toured the workspace, reaching out as if to touch a sculpture but then withdrawing. She was beautiful, wrapped in a black wool winter coat, her red curls danced around her face, framed by a colorfully handcrafted scarf with matching cap – much better than the hunter orange she'd sported the day she had walked uptown for the non-interview at the Chronicle. The day he'd given her a ride home. Home. Had Ashley begun to think of Miller's Bend as home? Would she be staying? He couldn't let himself feel any more for her until he knew.

"What do you think?" Matt asked quietly. "Do you like it?"

"Your work is … amazing," she replied as Ashley turned back to face him. He couldn't look away. "I had no idea you were an artist. It's just amazing."

Color tinged Matt's cheeks, either from the compliment, or because he realized that he'd been looking at Ashley far too openly. If she was paying attention, she could guess his feelings. "Thanks. I, ah …"

"Hope you like Mexican?" she asked as she raised the bag bearing their lunches.

He'd stepped close to Ashley and gently took the bag to set it on the table. And then, helping her shrug out of her coat, he answered, "I think the company is far more important than the food. Thank you for doing this."

With a quick "You're welcome," she began pulling entrees out of the bag from the drive-thru. She wondered at his words – was he simply thanking her for the food, or for something more? He excused himself to wash up and returned with a broad smile. "I'm really, really glad you're here," he said, as he pulled out a stool for her.

"I have news," she blurted before she could take a seat. She had to know if Mrs. Holmes was right – would her decisions matter to Matt. Looking up into his face, which had been so open and happy a moment ago, Ashley wondered how he would respond. Already, he seemed guarded, as if ready to close himself off and back away. "It's a good development, really. And I'm happy about it."

Don't say you're leaving. "Did you remember something? Is that it?" he asked hesitantly. "Maybe I was wrong … maybe I should tell you all about the evening when you fell …. Maybe it would help."

Ashley scowled slightly. "It doesn't matter anymore. Either I'll remember or I won't. But I've made a discovery and a decision."

"Okay," he answered slowly. "What is it?" He was definitely guarding his thoughts now, she realized. He didn't want to steer her decisions. She was thankful, but also wished he would give her a little inclination as to whether he cared if she stayed or left, if he cared about her.

"I've wished and I've hoped and I've prayed," she continued. "And I'm learning to listen. And I've learned to trust myself – at least in some areas. So … I'm here to celebrate the next step on my journey."

Ashley thought he actually paled slightly. He inhaled deeply and tipped his face skyward as he closed his eyes. "Your next step on your journey," he repeated quietly. Bringing his attention back to Ashley, he concluded, "So you're leaving."

She read sadness and regret in Matt's face before he turned away. "Oh, no. No, Matt." With his back turned, shoulders stooped, defeat in his bearing and posture, Ashley felt a sense of déjà vu. She had seen him like this before, but when?

She had a flash to the night of the wedding, the night of her fall. He'd been talking with a woman, out on the patio. The woman left him standing there alone and dejected. Who was the woman? Had they been lovers? The idea sickened her and raised a vile taste in Ashley's mouth.

Ashley mentally shook off the image, it didn't matter. *Now* mattered. She stepped quickly up behind him and laid a hand to his shoulder. "No. I'm staying."

He didn't turn to face her, but quietly laid out the words, "But for how long?"

"Please, Matt. Please look at me," she pleaded quietly. "I won't hurt you like she did."

He turned slowly, faced her and searched her face. Narrowing his eyes on her, he voiced single word: "Who?"

"The woman on the patio." Ashley swallowed hard, but held his gaze.

"When did you remember that?"

"Just now … when you turned away … it was so similar."

"She didn't hurt me," he began. Noticing the skeptical look in Ashley's expression, he clarified, "She was a friend. A friend I had hoped could be more, but neither of us felt that way after months of trying to."

"You looked hurt."

"I … was feeling sorry for myself," he explained. "Asking God why I couldn't find someone to build a real relationship with."

"And?"

"And He dropped you right in front of me … on the patio," he said with a sad smile. "He let me care about you when I didn't want to. And now you'll leave, too. Right?"

"No."

"No?"

"I'm staying in Miller's Bend. I'm making a life here," she said with conviction. Reaching up, she touched his cheek, and her voice quavered, "And I hope you are part of that life."

Matt's gaze intensified as her words began to break through his defenses. She would be staying. She had feelings for him. Ashley wanted him in her life. He lifted a hand and slid his knuckles gently along the delicate skin of her cheek until he slipped his hand around her nape. Each leaned in, closing the distance. Again, Matt was struck by how badly he wanted to kiss this woman. His focus dropped to her lips, but he didn't follow through on the implied wish. Instead he brushed a light kiss on her forehead before pulling her into his arms.

After a moment, he found his voice again. "Are you sure?" He didn't want to let her go, but she pushed back a bit to search his features.

"Sure of what? That I want to date you? Get to know you better? See what happens between us?"

He nodded. "Exactly. That's exactly what I want to know," he answered. "I don't want to misunderstand. I don't want to let my feelings for you grow, if that's not what you want."

"I am sure. You are kind and caring. You're always there for whoever needs you and you have a loving, giving spirit that I'm drawn to," she revealed.

Matt pulled Ashley into a tight embrace. Holding her close, he silently thanked God for giving Ashley the fortitude to come to him, to give them the chance to see what their relationship could become. Chagrined that he had hidden his feelings for Ashley, and wanting to be sure she understood his intentions, Matt spoke quietly, "I can't tell you how glad I am that you're staying in Miller's Bend. You've been direct and courageous, when I wasn't able to be. I was trying to keep my feelings in the background - pushed into the shadows."

A bubbling laugh escaped from Ashley's lips, though she tried to stifle it by covering her mouth with her hand. "I'm not those things. Not at all," she divulged. "Not really."

"You came here to tell me; to be sure I was clear that you were staying," he reiterated as he steered her toward the table and stool. "We'd better eat so you can get back to work, right? Or were you planning to stay here all afternoon?"

"I suppose we should," she replied as she settled on the stool. He placed her entree in the microwave for a quick rewarm and returned it to her. The microwave was now humming away as it warmed his meal.

"Now that you've said what you came to say -"

"Oh, no!" she interrupted. Swallowing the first bite of her lunch, she added, "I almost forgot … that's not *exactly* what I came to tell you."

"It's not?" Matt's expression shifted and his skin colored with a blush. Had he misunderstood – made a fool of himself? Ashley beamed at him with unfettered excitement and he felt his insecurity slip away a little. She'd made herself clear – she'd said she wanted to see what kind of relationship would develop between them. He pushed his thoughts back earlier in the conversation, she'd been pulling the entrees out of the bag and placing them on the table. She'd said that she had news … and he'd jumped to the conclusion that she would leave. Matt reminded himself that he would have to stop expecting the worst, at least where Ashley was concerned. The microwave dinged and he transferred his meal to the table.

"Are you ready for this?" she asked excitedly. "You'd better sit down."

"I think I'll stand," he replied dryly.

She cast him a look, sighed deeply and rose to her feet. “Fine. Then I will, too.” She stepped close him again. “I told you I had news. Well … here it is. I bought the Chronicle.”

She looked up at him – her face filled with joy. Complete happiness at telling him her news. He quickly tried to understand why she was telling him, what his response was supposed to be. What did she expect of him?

She clearly expected some sort of reaction, so he gave a cautious try to please her. “That’s great?”

The delight in her eyes dimmed dramatically at his response, and then she glanced away. “Oh.” She slipped back onto the stool and took another bite of her lunch. If she’d realized how this was going unfold, she would have grabbed cold sub sandwiches instead. Not wanting to reheat the food again, she wrapped it up and shoved it away.

“Hey? What’s the matter?” he asked, as he reached across the table to touch her hand.

“I thought …,” she paused. Inhaled and met his gaze before continuing, “I thought you’d be glad to know that I intend to stay here permanently.”

“I am glad for that,” he confirmed. “Just don’t know why you’d buy a business – that’s a big commitment to a town you’ve only visited. I hope it wasn’t a rash move. I hope you didn’t do it to try to prove something to me, or to anyone. And that includes yourself.”

“It wasn’t,” she replied. “I made the arrangements to buy the Chronicle *before* I lost my memory. Before I even met you. I had made arrangements for my belongings to be shipped to Shelby’s house. I had made my decisions, based on what was best for me. *Before* I met you.”

"Before?" His cell phone buzzed in his pocket, and Matt glanced at the clock on the wall. He needed to close up the studio and go pick up his mother.

"Yes. I found the documents in my belongings Monday night," she explained. Her words faltered as she recalled the fact that Catherine hadn't intended to interview her before putting Ashley to work. She also recalled the old woman's comment the first day they'd met, saying she hadn't expected to see Ashley so soon. The pieces were starting to fall together to make sense.

She picked up the conversational thread. Referring to the documents, she explained, "I took them to a lawyer Tuesday morning to be sure I understood the contents and he confirmed it."

"What lawyer?"

"Mason Alexander. Shelby recommended him," Ashley replied. "Why does that matter?"

Did you dance with him again? "It doesn't. He's a good lawyer," Matt answered. His phone buzzed again. "Look. I've got to go. I have an appointment."

"I need to get back to work, too." She reached for her coat, but Matt picked it up first. He held it while she slipped into it – feeling her warmth, feeling her hair tickle his hands. Matt knew he wanted to have a relationship with this woman. She turned to face him, her expression open and confident. "I'm glad we had lunch together," she said. "Even if we didn't get to eat. I think it was important to talk about things."

"Me, too," Matt answered. "I should have let you know that I've begun to care about you, but I didn't want to influence you." He pulled Ashley into his arms for a brief hug. His phone was buzzing again. Ashley pulled back as Matt said regretfully, "I'm sorry, but I really have to go."

Neither moved. "Are we still on for Friday evening?" she asked.

He hadn't thought about his other commitments when he'd made the date – he'd just been focused on seeing Ashley, and seeing her portfolio. Could he manage? He wanted to – needed to – see her. He'd make it work.

"Absolutely," he confirmed. He reached for his coat, flipped the lights off, and pulled out his keys. "I'll walk you to your car."

With the studio locked, he guided Ashley to her car. Before closing the door, he asked, "Can you do me a favor?"

"A favor?" she echoed as she looked up at him. "Sure. What is it?"

His breath caught as she waited. She was beautiful and sweet, and he was far too attracted to her. He shouldn't say it, it was too early in their relationship to be territorial, or jealous, but he couldn't stop the words. "Please avoid dancing with Mason again."

The look of puzzlement lasted only seconds before Ashley smiled broadly. And Matt realized in that instant that he'd said too much – she'd seen his insecurity – he'd given her the chance to hurt him. But then devilment danced in her eyes when she replied, "No problem. I'd rather dance with you any day."

She closed the door and backed the Trailblazer away. As the phone in his pocket began buzzing again, she smiled and waved, and then she was gone.

CHAPTER TWELVE

They say hindsight is 20/20. Chrissi was beginning to understand as she reflected on her situation and the steps that she had taken which led her to this place. She'd been certain that she knew what she was doing, how to proceed, and that she would succeed. But that was days ago – weeks ago, really, when it all began.

The realization that she had been incredibly naïve and unprepared for what she'd walked into didn't help resolve the situation. Chrissi was in big trouble. Wishing that she'd listened to her brother, or her father, didn't help. No one from home knew where she was; by now even her easy-going mother would have enlisted the help of the authorities, but they wouldn't know where to search for her. Her father knew she was headed to the Chicago area, but he didn't know why, and he wouldn't know the perilous circumstance Chrissi was in. She needed to find a way to escape – either with or without Maddy – and get to the police. Maybe she would be able to convince them to save Maddy.

She lay still, with her eyes closed, listening for sounds of movement. Who was awake? How many people were around? Was it safe to allow herself to stretch and move? There were various men who guarded the two women. One was vile and disgusting - Chrissi had arbitrarily named him Slug. Slug the Thug. Her stomach clenched every time he was present. And she particularly dreaded the hours he watched over them when the boss wasn't present. He scared Chrissi more than the man who held her and Maddy captive. The man in charge, the others just called him JT, was mean, but he was careful and he was smart. He had goals – was a businessman – and he seemed to have rules and boundaries. He was definitely a criminal, but he had restraint.

Chrissi felt a gut-deep instinct that Slug would do horrible things to her and Maddy if he wasn't so deeply afraid of JT. And it was fear, not respect, which kept Slug in his place. More motivation to escape before it was too late – or was it already too late? Chrissi had a niggling that the nightmares might not have been dreams. She shook off the feelings that accompanied those questions. She had to focus on getting out. She would deal with everything else later … when she was safe at home again.

Two of JT's "associates" looked like TV henchmen. They were stereotypical almost to the point of being humorous – except there was nothing funny about the situation. She'd named them Tweedle Dee and Tweedle Dum, mostly to give herself a reason to smile from time to time. She didn't think they cared one way or another about anything other than the tasks they were assigned by JT. If he said, "Watch her", they watched; if he said "Feed her", they brought food. She was afraid of what would happen if JT said, "Kill her."

Chrissi had been worried about her cousin, Maddy, and formulated the plan to "save" her from her boyfriend, JT. How many days had she been here? Three? Maybe four? She remembered how she had stupidly walked in and demanded to take Maddy with her. She was going to take her back to Miller's Bend and help Maddy get over the lousy relationship, get clean and sober, and start a new life. The first of several problems was that Maddy was too scared to go anywhere. Before Chrissi thought things through, she'd spouted threats about going to the police and found herself manhandled into a room that only locked from the outside.

The rest of the house was decent, but this room was bare. She assumed there was another similar room where Maddy was kept. There was one window which was covered with a security screen – apparently to keep intruders out, but it also assured that guests like Chrissi would stay put. There was one blanket and a can in the corner of the closet. A chain tethered Chrissi to the wall, helping reinforce the dictate that she wouldn't be leaving. The can needed to be emptied, but neither JT, nor three of the guards seemed to think that was a necessary step in keeping their guest comfortable. Only the fourth guard seemed to possess any compassion at all – and he carefully hid it if any of the others were present in the house.

She could easily hear them discussing business and plans if more than one was present anywhere in the little house, so she knew how they interacted with each other. The odd thing was that if Number Four was alone in the house with the captives, he would open the door to her cell – not let her out – but keep the door open for a while. He would give her more food than any of the others would for meals, he would empty the can, and he would stand outside the door and talk quietly. He revealed nothing personal, never wanted to know anything personal. But Chrissi had learned to listen for his voice, his footsteps, knowing that she would have a brief reprieve from the desolation if Number Four was left on duty.

That first night, when Chrissi had been locked in the desolate room and chained to the wall, she'd been defiant. When Slug delivered supper to her she'd been famished and had eaten the miserly portion with enthusiasm. She'd begun to feel strange – not like herself later – and had become nauseous and anxious. She prayed for help, and had begun reciting Psalms and other Bible verses as she waited. Slug would appear in the door way, leer at her in a way that made Chrissi wish someone – anyone else – was present. Even JT would have been preferable. She'd finally slept, but suffered horrific nightmares that she still didn't want to remember.

The door to her room had been opened and slammed shut the next morning, awakening Chrissi abruptly. Rough voices argued in the next room.

"What did you do?!"

"Same as you'd of done."

"You're nothing but an animal! I ought to kill you where you stand!"

"Try it. JT will skin you before lunch."

"I don't care! I find her like that again and you won't make it out of this house. Ever. Now get out of my sight."

Chrissi had been disoriented, still feeling slightly sick and sluggish. She'd slid into the corner of the closet and concealed herself with the blanket – as if that would camouflage her or protect her. She'd waited and waited, while repeatedly reciting in a whispered voice, "Take up the whole armor of God that you may be able to withstand in the evil day."

Presently the door had opened slowly. Chrissi had heard foots steps as one of the men moved closer, closer. She squeezed her eyes closed tightly, willing him away. A shuffling sound registered and she shivered. She'd heard similar sounds the night before in her nightmares. She imagined that he was very close to her, close enough to pull the blanket away and touch her if that was his intent. "Miss?"

Ridiculously, relief flashed through Chrissi. Relief that it was Number Four who stood in her room. Ridiculous, because he was still a captor, still a criminal, and she was no closer to freedom. Willing herself not to move, she waited.

She heard a deep sigh, and then she the sounds as he straighten and stepped back. "He won't do it again … not if I can help it. But you have to help yourself, too."

"How?" she asked in a strangled whisper.

Number Four stepped closer again and this time he did tug at the stained blanket, exposing the top of her head, and then her frightened eyes. He muttered an oath and the muscles in his cheeks flexed. Something dark and deadly moved over his features. Holding her gaze he advised, "Stay still and quiet. Don't draw attention to the fact that you're even here. And … for God sake, don't eat or drink anything he brings you. That's probably how he drugged you."

Eyes wide, Chrissi pulled at the blanket. "Drugged me?"

Number Four narrowed his gaze, "You didn't know?"

She simply shook her head.

He swore again as he reached into the pocket of his suit coat. "Here. Don't let them see this," he advised as he handed her a tiny Bible.

Tears filled her eyes. Unable to express the depth of her gratitude, she croaked, "Why?"

"It would expose me … we'd both be dead."

When he left the room, the door remained open.

Chrissi had devoured the Word, while Number Four remained at the house. He didn't return to her doorway until he delivered a meal shortly before one of the others would come to take over. She looked up as he paused, his gaze traveling the perimeter of the room. He scanned every surface before his dark gaze landed on Chrissi's face. "Where is it?"

"Sorry, sir, I've no idea what you're talking about," she replied in a quiet passive tone.

A hint of a smile played at the corners of his mouth and he gave a quick, confirming nod. "Good girl," he said so softly that Chrissi wondered if she'd heard him at all.

"When I asked you why earlier, I meant 'why did you bring it' …" she said almost inaudibly.

Number Four knelt beside her to set down the tray. "I've heard you. I thought it was the single most helpful thing I could bring you. Just don't let them find it," he warned again.

"It's safe," she assured him. "Thank you."

In the days since that encounter, Chrissi had begun to crave the times when Number Four would be her guard. And now, several mornings later, she waited, listening, hoping Number Four would be the one to come through the door. She held her body stock still. The lock turned, the door opened. No words … usually Number Four would speak soothingly to her as if she were a shy animal that would bolt. She tensed as she waited.

She felt the weight of a man's hand on her shoulder. Just as fear surged and her bile rose, she heard him whisper, "I'm sorry, but it's going to get worse, before it gets better."

The relief of hearing Number Four's voice conflicted with the words he spoke. "Worse?" she asked in a voice that cut out. "How can it get worse?"

"Bullets," he answered grimly. "I need you to stay down … and covered."

"Why not let me go?"

"Can't. This is the best I can do," he answered as he pulled a dark folded cloth from inside his jacket. "Hurry – get in the corner of the closet."

Chrissi scurried to comply, wondering what was going to happen. And how did Number Four have advance notice? He moved the can and handed the contraband Bible to Chrissi, who clutched it to her chest as she settled as deeply into the corner as she could. He draped the cloth over her before covering it with the loathsome blanket.

"What's this?" she asked, indicating the hidden layer.

"Ballistic barrier," Number Four replied, as if that was a complete answer in and of itself.

Chrissi's brows drew together before she asked, "A bulletproof blanket?"

"Not completely. We call it bullet-resistant," he said in explanation. "Keep quiet. When you hear a ruckus, get your head tucked under the barrier. And keep praying." He stepped away and passed quickly through the doorway. The door closed quietly and Chrissi heard the lock snick into place. Although this time it felt like it was for her safety, rather than for her confinement.

The "ruckus" began only moments later.

Two more days, and the countless interviews with police officers, detectives and special agents finally ended with Chrissi free to go. She would be called back to Chicago for the trial of JT and his associates who had been captured. A few had been killed in the melee, and a few, including Slug the Thug, had escaped capture. But law enforcement was counting the case as a major success in the battle against organized crime.

Maddy wasn't as lucky as Chrissi. The detectives determined that she had chosen to be affiliated with JT and his organization, and charges were filed against her in the case. She was considered a flight risk since Chrissi was adamant about taking Maddy home with her, and as a result, Maddy's bail had been denied. Chrissi planned to try again to get the judge to set bail, so Maddy could travel with her to Miller's Bend.

Although it pained her, Chrissi had convinced the authorities in Chicago to delay telling her family back home that she'd been found. She knew they were concerned and searching for her, but she was safe now. And besides, the story she had to tell would only worry them more – it must be told in person. Otherwise, they – at least Matt – would be on the next flight to Chicago, only to turn around and fly home again with her.

Chrissi would wait a few more days before making the trip home. A full day would be spent in travel and she would be escorted to Miller's Bend by agent Joseph Stockard, formerly known as Number Four. The pair was slated to travel together by plane to Sioux Falls, where they would rent a car for the remaining two-hour drive. Stockard would brief the local law enforcement officials, and then Chrissi would face her family.

CHAPTER THIRTEEN

The wind whipped at Ashley's hair as she huddled closer to the shelter of the door. She hated northern plains Januaries because they are so cold. Oh, sure, the weatherman finds a lot of other ways to say it, but it all boils down to the fact that they are cold. She knocked loudly on the pane of glass in the large wooden door. Only a few days remained until they would enter February, and the temperatures would moderate, but in the mean-time the weather conditions were brutal.

She stood shivering as she waited for Mrs. Gibson to open the door of the home at 1102 South Sixth Street, so she could get started on the second interview she had arranged for Friday. Since she began working at the Chronicle, Ashley had interviewed four of the "characters" on the list Catherine provided. She'd found all of the residents to be interesting and unique – there was a man who was passionate about collecting war memorabilia, a woman who had made it big in the movies and then returned to her hometown of Miller's Bend to live quietly when she decided the bright lights and fast life of fame were not God's plan for her, a woman whose grandmother had taught her the heritage art of Hardanger embroidery and her work was in rising demand all across the country, and the couple who had born and raised three sets of triplets.

And sure enough each of them mentioned in the course of their interviews that a daughter or a sister had disappeared inexplicably. Despite searching, praying and hiring detectives, they hadn't heard from the missing loved ones again – at least not for a few years. Ashley learned as much as possible about the run-aways without raising suspicions. And she'd learned that, in the cases so far, the girls had re-established contact with the families eventually.

She had written the light feature articles while each interview was fresh in her mind and cataloged the information about the run-aways to be studied later and brought together in a comprehensive in-depth piece. She realized that she would likely have to speak with the families again before completing that assignment. Ashley wondered whether the families she still planned to interview had also been lucky enough to reestablish contact with their daughters, or if some of the young women remained missing.

She raised her hand to knock again. If Melanie Gibson didn't answer this time, she would have to call and reschedule the interview. Before her knuckles made contact with the window pane, Ashley heard the faint sounds of someone approaching from inside the home. Stepping back and straightening, she looked up as the door opened.

"Good afternoon," she began automatically before realizing that she recognized the man who stood in the open doorway. Matt. Ashley's words died away as her mind scrambled to make sense of the scene. She hadn't seen Matt since Tuesday, although the two had talked on the phone each day. He'd explained that he was busy with work and some family issues. Matt had assured Ashley that he was looking forward to their date Friday evening.

Yet, here he was, lounging in the home of Mrs. Gibson in the middle of the afternoon. And, although he seemed strained, with dark rings beneath his eyes, Matt smiled broadly as he gazed at Ashley. He was dressed casually, in sweatpants and a University of Minnesota Morris T-shirt, and his hair was mussed, as though he'd just awakened. The thought of disturbing him when he was in bed thoroughly flustered Ashley and she felt the heat of a blush pushing into her cheeks. After a moment that seemed to stretch for an eternity, he spoke quietly, "You must be freezing out there. Come on in." Ashley had to admit to herself that she was indeed getting far too cold for comfort and casual conversation. Of course, words were still evading her as she stepped across the threshold.

"You're pretty early for supper," he said. He'd phrased it as a statement, but to Ashley's ears it sounded more like a question. It was her cue to offer an explanation for her presence in his home. She'd been invited for supper at six o'clock, and here she was at 3:30 – well 3:40. She was definitely late for her appointment with Mrs. Gibson – wherever she was. Matt rubbed his eyes wearily before moving into a stretch – the kind a person's body demands after a heavy sleep or hard work out. The motion revealed to Ashley the man's full height and breadth and she realized she had underestimated him on both counts. His stretch also revealed a strip of exposed skin above waistband of the sweatpants. Ashley's cheeks burned as she realized how easily the sight had drawn her attention.

Quickly looking away, she offered a weak response, "It was an accident. I guess I'm lost."

"Lost in Miller's Bend?" he retorted as he stifled a yawn. "Never thought I'd see the day."

Her brows furrowed in frustration. "I'm supposed to be at an interview with Mrs. Gibson – Melanie Gibson. I must have the address wrong," she said as she set her bag down and began rifling through it for the paper on which she'd penned the address. "I'll just call her and apologize for being late and get directions from here – she must be close by …"

Silently Matt had stepped closer to Ashley and now he reached out to touch her shoulder lightly, drawing her attention. "You mean you didn't come to see me?" he teased.

Ashley abandoned the search for the paper, turned to face Matt and looked up into those incredible crystal blue eyes. "This is serious," she explained. "I was supposed to meet Mrs. Gibson at 3:30 and I'm late – I have to call her."

Matt shook his head. "No, you don't. You're in the right place," he said. "Melanie is here, but she's resting. You can't talk to her now," he continued, as shadows of regret skittered across his features.

"Here?" The one-word question had slipped from Ashley's lips, but she'd managed to stop the other questions that threatened to tumble after it. *Who is she to you? Why is she here? You live with a woman – a married woman?* Disappointment sliced through Ashley as she backed away from Matt. She'd hoped for a relationship with him, but here he was sleeping in another woman's home. A sense of betrayal stabbed at her heart. She pulled her bag over her shoulder again, preparing to make her exit. "I see," she quipped coldly as she worked to cloak her emotions.

Ashley began striding toward the door. Anger and embarrassment burned through her system. He'd seemed like a genuinely nice guy, but now she knew the truth: He was a philanderer – and a two-timing one at that! Tears burned behind her eyes as she reached for the doorknob. When his words reached her, the impact stopped her retreat.

"No, Ashley. You don't see," he said roughly.

"Don't I?" she challenged.

And then more quietly, but with irritation and clear exasperation, he said, "You don't see at all. Are you so sure that you can judge the situation in a few seconds? If you are, then go ahead and leave." He paused and, against her will, tears glittered in her eyes when she whirled to face him. Matt's expression was quiet, his stance non-confrontational, his whole bearing could be described as humble, rather than arrogant or defensive. "Come on, Ashley." The words slipped softly from his lips. Matt stepped close to her again. "There are a dozen possible explanations for what's going on here. Aren't you open to any of them?" He opened his arms, silently inviting her closer.

Ashley's anger was easing, and she began to question her assumptions. His soulful, tired expression wasn't helping her hold onto the impression that she'd been deceived. It was Matt's humility that tipped the scales. She didn't want to step into the embrace though, not until she'd heard him out.

"I'll listen to your explanation," Ashley countered as she reined in her agitation. "But please understand how this looks from my side. You invited me here at six; I show up early by accident and you've got a Mrs. Gibson in your bed and you look all … rumpled … and exhausted," she said as she once again felt the burn of a rising blush her cheeks and the ripples of the pain of betrayal in her heart. The latter was ridiculous, of course, because neither owed the other any loyalty. They had only decided to try dating; they were just friends. Weren't they?

Annoyance, resentment and exasperation played across Matt's features. He looked a bit more awake now, but he still seemed irritated and maybe a little hurt. A sad, ironic smile lifted the corners of his mouth slightly as he stepped forward, closing in on Ashley. Even though he'd moved near enough to touch her, she felt secure and unthreatened. "So you think Mrs. Gibson and I have something going on?" he asked in serious tones. With a hint of playful teasing he added, "And if we did, why should that bother you?"

Why indeed?

"I …" Ashley had no answer. But the intensity of his crystal blue gaze had captured her fully. She couldn't think and she could barely breathe. She could hardly hold her ground as she peered up at him. He was much taller than she was and so close she felt as though he was pressing her back to the door, even though he hadn't touched her at all. Finally, she gasped, "Well? *Do* you have something going on with Mrs. Gibson?"

Matt shook his head before answering. "Shame on you," he replied as he stepped back. "Assuming things," he added and he began to smile as though he knew a secret. Ashley noted that Matt also was sporting the ruddiness of a blush and that his breaths were shallow.

"So, why don't you quit toying with me and tell me what's going on?" she asked with rising discomfort.

"Mrs. Gibson is *not* in my bed," Matt supplied as he lowered himself into a chair and indicated that Ashley should do likewise. "She's in her own bed," he said as his eyes locked on Ashley's. "Melanie is my mother."

Relief coursed through Ashley as she sighed, "Thank goodness." The relief was short-lived as a new volley of questions surfaced. The first in her mind was "Why would you live with your mother?" but she managed not to give voice to that one, at least not yet. "You said she's resting?" Ashley asked, hoping the answer would reveal something that would help her understand.

Matt had let his head fall back in the chair. His eyes had drifted closed - he was so tired. If only he had help … The idea might have been generated by his exhausted brain, or it might have been borne of divine intervention, but he pulled forward and gazed at Ashley for a moment before asking, "Could you stay? I'm about to collapse … I need just a short nap."

What exactly was he asking of her? "You want me to … do what?"

"Just stay. Listen for Melanie … if she calls for me, wake me up." He had captured Ashley's hand as he made his request. The warmth of his grasp was distracting. Ashley recalled her friends commenting that Matt takes responsibility for everybody and everything. They would often comment that he never allows anyone to help him. And yet, here he was … asking her to help; trusting her to help.

His hushed request touched her and she nodded in response. "Yes, I'll stay."

"Thank you," he whispered. He leaned back let his head drop against the back of the chair and his eyes drifted closed. He'd been taking care of his mom for what seemed like most of the previous 72 hours. It was his mission to take care of her, see to her needs, try to keep her comfortable, all while running the household and trying to accomplish his work responsibilities. Why had he thought he would have the strength for a date with Ashley? *Because I wanted a date with Ashley!*

"I'm sorry your mom is feeling poorly," she replied. Ashley leaned back in her seat, but didn't let go of Matt's hand as he drifted toward sleep.

"Maybe we should reschedule the date," he said softly just before the exhaustion overtook him.

Matt awakened groggily from the short sleep he'd had in the living room chair. In a mildly disoriented state, he'd been excited when he heard women's voices emanating from the kitchen – maybe Chrissi had finally come home. Maybe his mother had turned the corner and begun to feel better following the treatment. But as he leaned against the doorjamb at the entrance to the kitchen, he wasn't as disappointed as he should have been to see that it wasn't Chrissi, but Ashley, who wore his mother's apron. The guest – his date – was busy cooking up a storm while she chatted with his mother, who sat heavily on a stool at the island.

Melanie still showed the strain of her treatments and the exhaustion that lingered for days after each bout of chemo. She was wrapped in a robe and leaned against the countertop for support, but she was up. Thank goodness. Matt's mind moved back to the redhead who worked industriously in the kitchen. She'd stayed when he'd fallen asleep and apparently had cleaned the kitchen and begun preparing supper – the supper he was supposed to have ready. He snorted to himself as he realized what a horrible host he was.

The sound drew Ashley's attention and she glanced quickly toward him. Melanie's gaze followed the younger woman's and her face lit with love as she saw him. "Oh, Mathew! I'm so glad you're finally up, sleepy-head," she said, as she extended an arm toward him in a silent invitation for a hug. "We were beginning to think you would sleep there all night."

"Not a chance, Mom," he said quietly as he stepped forward and moved to hug his mother and drop a kiss to her cheek. "I see you and Ashley have met …"

"Yes, yes," Melanie answered. "We are getting along just fine." She patted him lightly and released Matt from the hug. He stepped back as his focus turned to Ashley. So many thoughts stampeded through his mind but none coalesced into words as he stared at the woman who looked so right in their home. She looked as though she belonged. "Don't you think you should get dressed for your date, dear? We girls can manage alone for a few more minutes," his mother prompted gently.

The threesome dined when Matt returned a short time later. He'd showered and changed and he felt much more alert and human than he had for the better part of the day. After supper, he escorted Melanie to her room, as she was once again exhausted. He returned to the dining table to find that Ashley had cleared it and was loading the dishwasher.

"Leave it," he said, speaking more gruffly than he'd intended. When she turned to face him, he saw that he'd hurt or at least confused her with his tone. "I'm sorry. I didn't mean it harshly," Matt hurried to explain. "It's just …" he stopped. Glancing around the kitchen he realized how much work she must have done while he was sleeping in the chair in the living room. "I'm embarrassed. I invited you over for supper and you end up cleaning and cooking for me while I sleep in the other room. You shouldn't have done that."

Ashley closed her eyes as the image of the sleeping Matt surged back to life in her memory. She'd stayed in the living room briefly, thinking that he might wake up. But watching him sleep, even for only a short time, had left her feeling as though they shared a level of intimacy that they shouldn't. She'd risen, moved to the kitchen where she had worked, until she'd heard Melanie calling to her son.

"Your mom was up almost the whole time I was here," she said as she closed the door on the dishwasher and rinsed and dried her hands. "We went ahead and did the interview while I was cooking. So it all worked out," she hurried on. "I'm not afraid to do a little work. It's nice to be useful."

The interview. The reason she was here was the interview – not Matt. The reminder irritated him to an unreasonable degree. "And just why are you interviewing my mother?" he asked as his lines in his face hardened. "She's very sick."

Taken aback by Matt's attitude, Ashley dropped her gaze to her hands which were twisting the towel in agitation. Shaking the towel out, she hung it over the bar to dry. "Yes, I know that … now," Ashley whispered. "Perhaps I should go …"

No! I need you. The thought whipped through Matt so quickly that it shocked him. "Wait, please," he said softly. When her gaze lifted to meet his, she saw the apology in his eyes and she knew in her heart that she had somehow become far too attached to this man. "I'm sorry. I shouldn't have been so gruff toward you," he offered. "I should be thanking you for taking over for me for a few hours. For helping Mom and for the cooking and cleaning you did."

He'd stepped close to her and now she tipped her face up to focus on his face, rather than on the muscular chest that was near eye level for her. She felt the pull of the attraction between them, just as she was certain Matt did, but neither of them acted on it. She could see that he wanted to take her into his arms; she desperately wanted to reach out to him, to hold him as well. Ashley stepped back, away from Matt. The spell was broken, or so she hoped.

Matt seemed embarrassed as he turned away, scrubbing his hands through his hair as he did so. With his back to her, he spoke in a low tone which reverberated somewhere deep in Ashley's soul. "I'd like to know what you and my mother talked about. What kind of story are you planning to write about her?" he asked.

"You're quite protective," Ashley observed.

Slight sarcasm tainted his reply. "You're quick." And then, because he knew he was being cantankerous, he revised his answer. "Sorry. Yes, I am very protective of the people I love. She's all I have right now and she needs me."

"Right now?" Ashley echoed. "What do you mean?"

His skin flushed. "Nothing. Never mind," he said as he turned toward the dishes she hadn't loaded into the washer.

"Oh, no you don't," she countered as she handed him the empty baking dish. "You opened this door. Now I think you'd better step on through it. What do you mean, by your statement?"

"Just what I said," he declared softly. "She's all I have right now."

"The rest of your family …?" Ashley's softly spoken query died away as she wondered how many people the gentle man before her had lost. "What's happened, Matt? You know I don't have a clue about your history."

"I know." At some point, he'd started a pot of coffee and now handed a cup to her as he gestured toward the living room. "I'll start at the beginning," he said as they settled side by side on the couch.

By the time he finished his story, Ashley's mind was swimming and her heart was aching for Matt. His biological father had died when Matt was eight. Melanie had been devastated and reeling from the loss, and had re-married too quickly. His sister, Chrissi, had been born before Matt turned ten; by the time he was in middle school, his stepfather had taken off. Melanie had divorced the man and taken her children on the road.

The little vagabond family had lit in Miller's Bend with the intention of moving on again. Something about the community had pulled them in and they'd finally settled down. This was home to Matt and his mother. But Chrissi had been plagued by unanswered questions and when she'd disappeared weeks ago, Matt assumed she'd gone on a quest for answers.

Her absence haunted Matt. He'd tried everything he could to get her to abandon her plan. He'd begged her to stay, tried to reason with her, tried emotional blackmail and had finally fallen back on forbidding her from going. The day after he had tried to dictate her course to her, she'd been gone. And he viewed it as his failing.

Matt related his surprise when Byron, his stepfather, had appeared at his studio recently with information about Chrissi. "I don't know what to do about him," Matt confided quietly to Ashley.

"Do? What do you mean?"

"I mean …" Matt began, but couldn't seem to find the words to continue.

The house was quiet. The refrigerator hummed in the other room; a clock ticked somewhere; and Ashley leaned closer to Matt as they sat, side by side on the couch. Uncertain of the turmoil Matt was attempting to unravel within himself, she felt that silence would be preferable to chatter. She interlaced her fingers with his, and waited.

"Byron wants to be part of our lives again," he finally revealed. His voice was low and rough. "I don't know if I can trust him enough to let him in. I want to protect Mom and Chrissi from the kind of devastation he caused when he left us."

"You can't," she said softly. "You may not like this, but they are able to make those decisions for themselves. You can love them and support them, but you can't dictate who they let into their lives."

A low growling grunt emanated from Matt as he looked away. "We trusted him. We needed him and he left us. You don't know what it takes to keep that pain buried. If he comes back …"

"You'll have to deal with it," Ashley replied. "Matt, you are clearly a person who loves deeply, fully, with your whole being. Because of that, you are extremely careful, before you let yourself love, but once you let yourself, your emotions lead you, guide you … define you."

"I trusted him when I was ten, and he abandoned us."

Tears stood in Ashley's eyes when he faced her again. "You loved him when you were ten … and you're afraid you still do," she said softly. "They were young – they were both under a lot of stress. And they were both mourning with the death of your father, right? They probably both made mistakes back then. Doesn't Byron deserve a chance?"

Matt didn't answer, and Ashley knew he'd exhausted the topic. At some point during the conversation, Ashley had snuggled close to Matt, who had naturally wrapped his arm around her to pull her even closer. Her heart twisted in sympathy for the tender-hearted man beside her as well as for the sweet boy he'd surely been. She longed to offer words of comfort, but none came to mind. Without warning, she laid a hand to his cheek and lightly kissed his lips.

CHAPTER FOURTEEN

"Dude!" Tyler's voice interrupted Matt's thoughts as he felt the screaming burn of the muscles in his thighs and calves. It hadn't even been two whole days since Ashley kissed him and he hadn't been able to center his thoughts on anything but her. He had no idea why he had given in and told her all about his past – and his present for that matter. He'd hoped that a good workout would help him refocus, so he could get back to his life. He had commissioned statuary that he needed to complete, a sister to find and a mother to take care of. He didn't need the distraction of a relationship, and yet, he was excited at the prospect of seeing Ashley again.

The sweat soaked his shirt front and back as he'd tried to work through his intensifying feelings for the mystifying Ashley Nelson. After hearing Tyler's yell, he shortened his stride to slow his pace and felt relief throughout his system.

Tyler pulled up beside Matt. "I thought you wanted to work out *together*," he wheezed as he caught up with his former roommate and long-time friend. "You're running like the devil himself is after you," Tyler said between breaths as the pair slowed to a walk. Although they were alone on the elevated track inside the only fitness facility in Miller's Bend, other patrons utilized the swimming pool, racquetball courts and gym.

The two had shared an apartment until Melanie needed her son at home again to help her during the days of chemo treatments and recovery. Tyler understood Matt, but when he didn't respond, Ty was at a loss. "What's eating you?" he demanded. "Is it Chrissi? Did you find her?" He didn't look at Matt as he asked, but directed his gaze out the window instead.

Matt shook his head in response as he drew in a deep breath. Finally stopping to face each other, he answered, "Erik said they are very close. He hopes to have better news by Monday. Or maybe Tuesday." Tyler's expression darkened, startling Matt when he saw a flash of fury.

"They aren't doing enough! This has dragged on too long - how can you be so patient? I'd be …" Tyler let his words trail away and reined in his irritation. Turning away, he began walking. Tyler tried again to get to the heart of Matt's current mood. He asked, "Is it your mom? Is she worse?" He was considerably shorter than Matt and, even though he was muscular, Tyler didn't run regularly, so he was still breathing hard.

"She's about the same," Matt supplied. "Tries to be upbeat."

"Okay." Tyler shrugged it off and started walking again. He was going to be sore from this round of exercise, no matter what he did. But, he knew that walking for a while to cool down would be helpful. Matt was beside him in a few strides. Lately when Matt was pensive like this, he was worried about the women in his life – his sick mother or his missing sister. He hadn't seemed all that upset when Lauren had left town, but Tyler thought, maybe his feelings were just starting to catch up with him.

"Is this about Lauren?" Ty asked quietly.

Matt cast a sideways glance, “Lauren?” he asked in a confounded way. “What about her?”

“You miss her?”

He made a sour expression as he considered the question before giving a negative head shake. “No more than I’d miss you if you left,” he answered with a grin. “Why would you think that?”

Tyler regarded his friend for a moment. “Well, some people would be upset if they got dumped during a wedding reception,” he finally suggested. “But not you?”

“We were friends,” came the curt reply. “Nothing more.”

They continued around the track until they came to the entrance. Each slipped on his coat, grabbed his gear, and then swigging from his water bottle, Tyler tried again. “Who is it?” he asked as they crossed the frozen parking lot.

“Who’s what?” Matt asked absently.

“I’ve had better conversations with my dog,” Tyler called over his shoulder as he headed toward his pickup. “Let me know if you ever decide you want to talk about it.” Matt watched as Tyler jumped into the truck, slammed the door shut and revved the engine, wondering if his friend would remember that Matt needed a ride home.

He didn’t.

The pickup sped from the parking lot with Matt looking after it. He zipped his coat, shouldered his bag a little higher and began walking. He’d be frozen when he got home, but he probably deserved to get sick, he thought to himself as he crossed the main artery through town. He’d been difficult with Tyler and he knew it, but something in his friend’s expression when he’d asked about Chrissi wasn’t sitting right with Matt. He couldn’t put his finger on it, but it bothered him. Matt had one more reason to find his little sister and get some answers from her.

He'd maneuvered about six blocks on the snow-packed sidewalks, wishing that he'd been the one who had driven to the fitness center so he could have ditched Tyler, when he heard a vehicle slow down behind him. As it pulled even, he recognized the driver as Riley, with Shelby in the passenger seat. She'd rolled the window down and been rewarded with a wintry blast of air. With a shiver she called to him that they'd pick him up at the next intersection.

The blue minivan pulled onto the next side street and parked. *Minivan. That's what happens when you get a wife and kids. You lose your cool ride, your freedom, your identity.* The thought passed quickly when he remembered the adoring looks Shelby often bestowed on Riley. He also remembered the difficulties they'd encountered in admitting they loved and needed each other; and the time that they'd almost drifted apart. Riley and Shelby were good together, he thought. Solid and stable, that's what a marriage should be. *Love and stability. That's what you gain when you get a wife - if God shows you the right woman.*

As he drew near the van, the side door slid open. Baby Isabelle cried out as the cold air hit her, and her cry startled her twin, Jacob, making him fuss. Not wanting to prolong the exposure of the babies to the cold air Matt dove into the van as the door began to slide closed. He figured he could land quickly on the back seat, but when he tipped his head that way, he found Ashley scooting over to make room.

"Hi," she said quietly with a blush rising in her cheeks. Clearly she remembered the closeness they'd shared … and the kiss.

Matt felt the heat in his face as he paused. “Hi,” he answered before he managed to drop into the seat beside her.

He heard Shelby say something, but couldn’t tell what it was or didn’t care. He was enraptured as he watched Ashley. Remembering the way she’d snuggled up against his side after supper Friday night made him wish he could hold her now. She’d been kind and understanding, listening as he talked about his childhood, his sister and his mom. She’d been supportive, but still unafraid to raise points he hadn’t considered, when he talked about Byron.

And he hadn’t been able to shake her out of his thoughts since.

Without a conscious decision, he reached across the short seat and lightly skimmed Ashley’s cheek. A startled peep and gasp escaped her lips as Ashley clutched his icy hand within both her warm ones, and pulled it away from the delicate skin. Her wide-eyed expression sought his and when their gazed caught, she exclaimed, “You are frozen! How far did you walk in this weather?”

She was taking care of him again – rubbing his hands, holding them, blowing her hot breath over them – trying to warm him. And it was working.

“Ash …”

“Hmm?”

“Maybe you should just *hold* them,” he whispered roughly.

Her eyes met his and Ashley noted an unsettling expression. Her breath caught in her throat and she dropped his hands. She felt the warmth of a blush rising in her cheeks and turned to face forward again. It was then that Ashley realized Shelby had been chattering away the whole time.

Matt leaned slightly in Ashley’s direction and captured one of her hands in his. “I didn’t say that I didn’t like it,” he teased as he tugged her closer to his body. She scooted over in compliance and when she glanced up again, she saw that Shelby had turned to face them.

Shelby, who had asked a question of one or both of them and not having heard a response, turned in the passenger's position and opened her mouth to repeat herself. She stopped suddenly as her gaze ping-ponged from one friend to the other. And Matt could see it happening, before a sound came from Shelby, he knew that she'd figured it out.

"Oh, my goodness!" Shelby squealed. "You two?"

Matt smiled and pulled Ashley closer. *Yes,* he thought, *we are a couple. And it feels right.* Shelby squealed again but it wasn't words this time – just noise. And then, although she was only inches from his ear, she all but yelled to her husband, "They're dating!" Riley's focus flew to the rearview mirror, where he connected with Matt and Matt could tell that his friend was grinning widely.

Shelby's next outburst was directed at Ashley: "Why didn't you tell me?!"

Matt slipped quietly into the house he'd grown up in, hoping he wouldn't disturb his mother if she was resting. The ride home hadn't been awkward after he and Ashley revealed that, yes, they were going to see if a relationship would develop. What would happen with their relationship? Would it be the real thing? Would it endure or would it end with her leaving him? *Even if she doesn't leave town, things still might not work out between us.* He dropped his gear bag and hung his coat in the closet. And then muttering to himself, "I'll probably end up with a broken heart," he turned to head for the shower. He found his mother regarding him quietly from the recliner where she'd apparently been seated the whole time. Had she heard his words? She gave no indication.

"Did you have a nice workout?" she asked. His shirt clung to his body and goose bumps were still standing out on his skin, even after riding the last few blocks in the warmth of the van. A shiver ran through his body before he could answer. "Mathew? What happened to you?" Melanie demanded as she rose and came to him. "You're frozen! Get a hot shower and I'll make you a hot drink for when you're out." Another shiver rattled down his spine as he nodded and headed for the shower.

"I think I'll hire a babysitter," Melanie said as she handed him a steaming mug of hot chocolate with marshmallows a short time after he'd showered and returned to the kitchen.

"A babysitter? For who, Mom?" he asked with a grin. "Is there something you're not telling me?"

Swatting her son lightly on the shoulder, she replied, "For myself." After a pause, she explained, "You're too busy. You have your work, and you are taking care of everything here. Then in the days following my treatments, you hardly get any sleep at all. It's just too much to ask."

"No, Mom," he said as he reached for her hand. "It's not too much. And it's my responsibility. I will take care of you."

"Someone else can do that. I need you to meet your work responsibilities and to find your sister," she spoke clearly. "Those are things only you can do."

Matt didn't want to argue with his mother. He decided that she could hire all the babysitters she wanted to; he would just send them away until she gave up. He would take care of her.

Matt woke up the next morning – sort of – feeling as though a Rottweiler was sitting on his chest. He hadn't slept well and was struggling to get his mind working. His sinuses were full and his head ached and it was hard to breathe. He pushed himself into a sitting position and swayed slightly. Influenza.

He looked at the clock and tried to focus as his head pounded. His mom was scheduled for another treatment today and he was in no shape to escort her. He was in no shape to care for her during the recovery days either. He needed help. *Now what, Lord?*

Maybe coffee would help. Coffee and pain relievers. Trying to ignore the pain in his achy muscles, he headed down the hall leading to the kitchen. His legs moved as if they were coated in lead and he felt like he weighed a few hundred extra pounds. When he entered the kitchen, he wanted to turn and run. Either hallucinations had begun to plague him or his mother's babysitter had arrived … and she was Ashley.

She raised her head from the task she was performing and a broad smile lit her countenance. It was like seeing an angel first thing in the morning and for a fleeting second, Matt thought it was the sight he'd like to see every morning for the rest of his life. And then something shifted inside his sinuses, his throat tickled and he began a spasm of coughing.

The image of the woman in the kitchen transformed immediately. Horror shown in her eyes as she rushed toward him with a towel in hand. She pushed it into his hand and lifted his hand to cover his mouth. "You look terrible," she said unnecessarily as she began to spin him to head back the way he'd come. "You can't be out here exposing Melanie to whatever you've got."

"I've got to take her for her treatment today," he argued weakly. He tried to turn back toward the kitchen, but Ashley deftly turned him toward the bedroom again. Matt paused to lean against the door frame of his room. In a back corner of his mind, he knew Ashley shouldn't follow him into the room. "I'm fine," he croaked, hoping she would leave him alone and go back to the kitchen.

"You're not fine. Get back in bed," she ordered as she slipped under his arm and steered him none too gently toward the bed with covers thrown back.

"Kind of bossy for a little thing, aren't you?" he countered. He was rewarded for his effort with another coughing fit and a dark glare from Ashley.

"You're not fit to take Melanie anywhere," Ashley declared. "Now get back into that bed."

"I will," he growled as he broke away from her grasp. She looked startled by his tone and stopped trying to handle him. Even in Matt's muddled state, he regretted that he'd spoken more sharply than he should have. "Wait," he said more quietly.

As he turned and sat down on the edge of the bed, he raised his face to meet Ashley's gaze. "I'm sorry I snapped at you," he wheezed. "I should be taking care of my mom." He paused and let his gaze drop before he continued in a voice barely above a whisper, "And you shouldn't be in my room."

Ashley's surprise at the harshness of Matt's voice when he'd broken free of her grasp passed quickly and as he spoke, she realized he was disappointed in himself and embarrassed. She thought moving past the moment would be best. "I'll bring you some breakfast … toast and juice? And some pain reliever," she said quickly.

"Just take good care of Mom, please," he said before he turned away and pulled the blankets over his body.

He dozed and awoke to find a tray with orange juice, a cup of coffee and a cup of water that were all the same temperature, a bottle of pain reliever and two slices of toast that were hard and dry. She'd sneaked back into his room. He was irritated and grateful. He downed the toast with the water and chased it with the juice before collapsing back into sleep.

And he dreamed.

In the way a person's mind twists the realities and suspends time, he dreamed of all those he'd loved. And in the dream they all became young adults at the same time: his dad and step-dad, his mom, his sister, and he are all equals. In dream-world it seems they all live together in a tiny little shack on an island that is no more than a mountain rising from the water. The mountain begins to rumble and spew lava. Everyone panics.

Matt's Dream-Dad runs up the mountain to try to stop the flow of lava – a fool's mission if ever there was one. *NO! Dad! Stay with Mom! Help Mom!* Matt's subconscious screams.

Crying and calling out after him, Dream-Mom scrambles away, chasing up the path he'd taken. Leaving Matt cowering – alone and frightened. The volcano growls and begins to twist and surge. Rocks fly from its mouth. The heat of the lava causes the sweat to break out, soaking Matt's skin and hair.

Suddenly Dream-Step-Dad, draped in Superman's cape, flies after Melanie. "I will save you all!" he declares before disappearing into the ash that's falling like snow down the mountainside. Hopelessness and coldness sweep over Matt. Shivering and desperate, he looks to the mountain and then to the sea on the other side of the hut. The sea is safer, he knows. But he cannot swim.

Someone pulls at Matt. "What will we do if they don't come back?" Chrissi wails as she grasps at his shirt. She's touching his face and he pulls away. He can't take care of her – he can barely take care of himself. "Dad! Mom! Help us!" he yells toward the mountainside. And he swims despite the fact that he doesn't know how; he swims hard away from the hut, away from the island. He swims, but Chrissi is pulling him down pulling, pulling, pulling ...

"Matt! Matt!" a voice calls from the shore and he turns toward the sound. The image of a woman wavers there on the shore, fading and reappearing. Fading and reappearing, and then she calls softly, "Matt, come back to me." He sinks below the choppy water's surface. "Matt."

Slowly he breaks the surface, gasping for air, and thrashing wildly. He mumbles, "Have to help them …"

"Matt. It's okay," a soothing voice speaks softly, as fingers tenderly brush his temples. "It's okay. I'm here. I'm here to help."

Clasping her hand in his, he pulled his eyes open. The dream had ended and the face peering down on him belonged to Ashley. Red hair formed a halo around her beautiful face and her blue eyes reflected concern. One hand gently stroked his cheek as she watched him closely. "You okay?" she asked with great seriousness.

Waiting for the sense of reality to return, Matt, nodded slightly. He wasn't drowning, at least not in water, and that was good. But he feared it wouldn't be long before he was drowning in emotions that centered on Ashley. Forcing his mind to focus elsewhere, he asked, "What time is it?"

Ashley frowned, thinking that he had no need to know the time, until she realized that his concern would be for his mother. "It's afternoon. Melanie had her treatment and we're back," she offered with a smile. "She's doing fine so far, but said I should expect her to get extremely tired starting about supper time or a little after. Does that seem right to you?"

He nodded. "Thank you," he breathed.

CHAPTER FIFTEEN

"How long have I been out?" Matt asked the next time he was sure he was seeing a real, live Ashley at his bedside.

"Long enough that we've started calling you Rip Van Winkle," she replied with laughter dancing in her eyes. She touched a hand delicately to his forehead and cheeks. He knew she'd performed the same test several times while his system fought the virus that had incapacitated him. But this time it felt different, probably because the fever had broken and he was on the road to recovery.

Without considering the consequences, he reached up and gently cupped her cheek. "Are you okay?" he asked. "You look exhausted."

She leaned lightly into his palm, letting her eyes drift closed. "I could use a little rest," she conceded at last. "It's been a long couple of days. I don't know how you've been handling it all these weeks," she concluded.

"You've been taking care of two of us," he pointed out. "That's harder than just taking care of Mom." Ashley realized that she was sitting on the edge of his bed, leaning into his gentle touch. It felt good and right.

She jerked away from his touch and lurched to her feet. "I'd better check on her," she said as she bolted for the doorway. Pausing she asked, "You'll come to the kitchen for supper?"

"Not if Mom's there – I don't want to risk infecting her," he said. And then with concern etched in his features, he added cautiously, "You've been careful? I mean going between us? Her immune system is compromised."

"Yes, I've been careful," she replied. "She's a great lady." Ashley walked toward the bathroom to wash before she headed to Melanie's room. She reflected on what she'd learned: Patients who receive chemotherapy treatments for cancer face a high risk for developing infections. Their bodies may be less able to fight infections once they develop. White blood cells are important in preventing and fighting infections. The chemotherapy damages their immune systems by lowering the number of white blood cells produced.

Survival rates for non-Hodgkin's lymphoma (NHL) vary widely, depending on the lymphoma type, stage, age of the patient and other variables. According to the American Cancer Society, the overall 5-year relative survival rate for patients with NHL is 63% and the 10-year relative survival rate is 51%.

Because the outlook varies so widely, making a definite prognosis is very difficult. And, although survival rates for patients with NHL have greatly improved since the early 1990s, especially for patients under age 45, Matt was looking at nearly even odds that he would lose his mother to the disease eventually.

Something twisted in Ashley's heart. Sweet, kind and loving Matt might suffer through the loss of his mother in addition to the losses of his father, stepfather and missing sister. *How much do you expect him to endure alone, Lord?* The thought had morphed into a prayer and the feeling that Ashley sensed in the next moment frightened her more than she would ever admit to anyone: *Matt's not alone – you are with him.*

Matt sat patiently at the kitchen table waiting for Ashley to return. Melanie had decided to stay in her room for supper, keeping her distance from Matt and the virus he might still harbor. They all agreed that he probably wasn't contagious anymore, but a few more hours of distance as a safety precaution was probably not unreasonable. Ashley would stay one more night and then return to her apartment at Mrs. Holmes' place.

Minor changes had occurred while Matt was down with the flu. The red-headed caregiver had claimed counter space in the bathroom, set up an office of sorts in a corner of the living room and had been cooking up a storm. She explained that the freezer was stuffed with frozen casseroles, divvied into containers with two servings each, so he'd have emergency meals when taking care of everything was just too much.

He marveled that she'd had time to cook and clean while caring for the both him and his mother. His gaze wandered back to the office area she'd established. Had she done some writing, too? Was she neglecting details at the Chronicle to help his family?

Ashley, returning to the kitchen from Melanie's room, paused in the hallway. Matt was well again, she thought as she watched him silently. His fever was gone, as was the glazed look he'd had when he'd awakened periodically the past couple of days. Although he had showered, shaved and cleaned up, he was still tired and weak. But by tomorrow, she figured, he'd be able to do without her assistance.

Matt insisted on cleaning up the kitchen after supper, while Ashley settled at her computer to write one of the stories that

Catherine had originally assigned her when she began working at the Chronicle. She delved into her work and was lost in thought when, about a half-hour later, she realized Matt was standing very close … way too close behind her chair. Reflex had her snapping the top closed on her computer and simultaneously whirling in her chair to face him. He'd been bent down, so he could read the type on her screen and now they were face to face. Mere inches separated them.

Ashley's quick words died on her lips as Matt's compelling blue eyes lit with something she hadn't seen in him before. Was it desire or an intense curiosity? Their gazes held each other captive, until his began a slow exploration of her face. And yet, she didn't move. As he leaned nearer, Ashley hoped he would kiss her again. And she hoped he wouldn't.

Matt's conscience kicked in just a moment before he'd have kissed Ashley. He shifted slightly and brushed her cheek with his lips, and closed his eyes tightly, as if to lock the image of woman forever in his mind. Straightening and taking a step back he asked, "Why did you do that?" He nodded vaguely in the direction of the laptop.

Ashley's mind was spinning. Worse yet, her pulse raced and her breath had turned shallow. "Do … what?" It wasn't much in the way of comebacks, she admitted to herself as she swallowed the disappointment caused by Matt's retreat.

"You closed the lid," he replied with a frown. "I was reading your story."

She turned back to face the computer, opening the laptop as she did. "It was just a reflex, I guess," she answered apologetically. "I don't think I've been like that before – secretive. But I have a feeling that Neal's been sneaking into my stuff and I suspect he's even been on my computer when he thinks I won't notice," she explained. With a frown, she looked back up into Matt's face. "I know it sounds paranoid," she added with a shake of her head.

Matt shrugged. "You never did show me your portfolio," he said in a blatant change of subject. "Do you have some of your work here - that you would allow me to see?"

"You don't mind that this story isn't ready to be seen?" she asked as she gestured toward the type on the screen.

"I understand," he confirmed. And she instinctively knew that he really did understand.

Ashley pulled some files from her bag and standing, she handed them to Matt. "You can look through these while I finish up here," she suggested. Regarding him a moment longer, she asked, "Your mom is worried that you aren't getting enough time to work on your sculptures. Do you need me to stay with her tomorrow so you can work?"

He gently laid the folders on a nearby table as he extended his hands in front of him, palms up. "I don't think I'll be steady enough yet tomorrow," he answered quietly. His hands shook slightly with the effort to hold the position. "That virus really wiped me out," he said with exasperation.

Taking one of his hands into her own, she felt the weight and warmth of it. As she studied it, she thought of how the sculptor's hand has incredible strength, while still being gentle. Her mind made the leap, comparing his hands to the spirit of the man before her – he was indeed filled with an abundance of strength and gentleness. As she lightly traced the outline of Matt's hand and then the lines of his palm, she began to understand how deeply she wanted to stay with him. Stay forever. To be held in those hands and in Matt's heart would be everything she'd ever need, short of heaven.

The light touch of Matt's fingers against her cheek startled Ashley. She'd been lost in exploring the hand she held, and her thoughts of forever. He'd slowly brought the other hand to graze her skin, setting off tingles in the wake. Slowly, his fingers slid into her hair at her nape and he nudged her closer to him. And just before their lips met, she saw in his eyes that he felt the same impression of forever with her that she'd sensed with him. They were in big, big trouble.

They clung to each other for a long time after the kiss ended – swaying slightly and bobbing in a sea of emotions. Neither spoke as they held on to each other and Matt knew without question that he wanted Ashley to stay with him. Stay for the long haul. He wasn't thinking about tonight or tomorrow. He was thinking about months and years down the road. And he knew, with a certainty he'd never felt before, that this woman he held in his arms was the one he would always love and never forget.

That's what he felt for her - love. He tightened his hold on her as he let the realization course through his mind and his heart. Pulling back, he gazed into her eyes, and he knew that he couldn't stop himself from loving her.

Ashley didn't know what to do with her emotions as they swam through her mind. She had been afraid that she was falling for Matt, with his tender, giving nature. But now she knew for certain that she was in way too deep. If this relationship failed, it was going to hurt tremendously. It might even break her heart. And from what she'd seen in his eyes and felt in his kiss and the way he held her, it might break his heart, too.

He pulled back, cupped her face in his hands and dropped one more kiss lightly on her lips before he walked away, without a word, toward his room. She watched his retreating form with rising regret. Should she follow him? Had she really seen the shimmer of tears in his eyes? What was he feeling?

Only seconds had passed after he closed the door between them when he heard the light knock. "Matt?" she whispered.

Oh, Lord.

"Don't open that door, Ashley," he growled in response. His voice conveyed a warning that she knew should not be ignored. It wouldn't be the same to walk into his room now as it had been when he was sick. Not the same at all, and yet …

Confusion sounded in her voice as she spoke again. "We should talk."

"Not now." His voice was gruff. If he saw her again tonight, he'd want to hold her. If he held her he'd want to kiss her. If he kissed her, he'd want to keep her … forever. "Please go away," he choked. *Please stay.*

"Oh. Okay." She sounded bewildered. Sad. "I'm sorry."

He heard the rattle of the door knob as she released it and then another faint "I'm sorry" before her steps retreated down the hall. "I am, too," he sighed. "I am, too."

He was even sorrier in the morning. He hadn't slept well and he'd decided that Ashley was right - they did need to talk. But she was gone. Her cosmetics and her temporary office supplies were gone and so was she. Well, he had asked her to go – what had he expected?

Mrs. Holmes answered the light rap at her kitchen door to find Ashley huddled close to the wall in the early morning light. The sun struggled to crest the horizon and the temperature had plunged in the pre-dawn hours. "Goodness, child. Come in, come in!" she exclaimed as she pulled the young woman into the enveloping warmth of the kitchen. "What in heaven's name are you doing out there?"

Ashley didn't have time to answer as Mrs. Holmes guided her to a seat at the kitchen table. Almost instantly, a cup of coffee accompanied by a fresh-from-the-oven caramel roll appeared in front of Ashley. "Thank you. It looks like you've been up for a while," she said.

Mrs. Holmes settled into an adjacent chair and watching Ashley she replied, "It looks as if you've been up for a while, as well." Ashley pulled a piece of the roll free and popped it into her mouth. Her hostess watched intently for a moment before she prompted. "You want to tell me what's going on?"

"I think …," Ashley paused, took a swallow of coffee and looked away. "I think I may need to leave …"

"Why would you think that?"

"I don't want to hurt anybody," Ashley said as though trying to convince herself.

"Anybody? If you leave, you'll hurt yourself, your friends, and your business. And probably, you'll hurt Mathew the most. And, isn't that really who you think you're trying to protect," the old woman guessed. "You two have realized that you have feelings for each other?"

Ashley nodded.

"I don't understand why you would want to leave … especially now that you know that Mathew cares about you," Mrs. Holmes pondered. "I would think that would be the icing on the cake, so to speak."

Taking a sip of coffee, and another bite of the steaming caramel roll, Ashley stalled for time. She realized that she hadn't felt lonely for even one minute since she'd been in Miller's Bend. She had re-connected with Shelby and Allison, and had forged friendships with their friends. She'd purchased a business and was establishing herself as a trustworthy journalist to the local community – a community where crime was nearly non-existent. And she'd fallen in love. Yes, that was the icing on the cake, as Mrs. Holmes said.

"But it's all happened too easily," Ashley finally confided. "Nothing good comes easy."

Mrs. Holmes swatted the air between them dismissively. "Oh, that's rubbish! I suppose you think that if things are going badly, you should just fight harder to hold your head above water, rather than changing course?"

The younger woman narrowed her gaze as she looked into her hostess' face. "You said that when you went away when you were young, you had to fight for everything – for your education, for your job and for advancements. You know as well as I do that is a harsh world out there." She paused, wondering if her next words would insult Mrs. Holmes. "Isn't it a little too easy to just live here in a quiet little town on the plains, run a little business and fall in love with one of the neighborhood boys? Isn't there some kind of payback for things going that well?"

Mrs. Holmes straightened in her chair and lifted her chin before replying. "I know *better* than you do, young lady – I went out and made my mistakes. I've lived with them and the repercussions of my decisions. But I have never once regretted returning to Miller's Bend – I have never regretted that I finally opened myself to heeding God's urging and returning to the place I belonged all along."

"But you have regrets?" Ashley inquired.

"Oh, yes," the old lady answered. Her silver-gray eyes were haunted when she looked into Ashley's face and grasped her hands. "But only one of them happened after my return to Miller's Bend."

"I don't know what to do," Ashley confided as she stirred her coffee before taking another drink. "I … Matt … He's confusing me," she finally said in exasperation. "He's so sweet and tender," she said, remembering the way he had kissed her and held her. She felt her skin heat with a blush and looked away. The sun had crested the horizon and its rays shimmered on the snow. A new day. Maybe something would happen today that would help her decide. Something besides Mrs. Holmes telling her that having Matt's affection was icing on some figurative cake.

"He cares for you; you care for him. So what's the confusing part?" the hostess asked with a smile.

"He told me to get out," Ashley responded flatly.

"That's odd, indeed. Not like Mathew at all …"

"I thought that, too. I think that's why it surprised me," Ashley responded. "We were so close … and then he just walked away."

"Where'd he go?"

"His room," Ashley answered. "I knocked on the door because I thought we should talk. He told me to go away."

Mrs. Holmes laughed out loud as she set her coffee aside and grasped Ashley's hands. "Oh, that's great news!" she crowed. "Great, indeed."

"It isn't," Ashley asserted.

"It is," the other woman proclaimed. "Don't you see? It would have been very inappropriate …"

Ashley's eyes had widened and her mouth dropped open. "I did not intend to go into his room. I just wanted to talk to him."

"Also good to hear."

"Stop it," Ashley beseeched. "I was confused and I wanted answers … but he shut me out!"

"Answers were what you wanted," Mrs. Holmes said as she nodded in agreement. "But did you ask yourself what Mathew wanted?"

With rising frustration, Ashley thumped her hand on the table. "I was trying to get him to tell me what he wanted."

"Don't you have brothers?"

The question threw Ashley for a moment. *Brothers?* "Well, yes. I have two brothers," she confirmed. "What's that got to do with this?"

"Male behavior, my dear," Mrs. Holmes said. "What do your brothers do when they are upset, or confused, or frustrated, or maybe even a little overwhelmed? Do they sit down at the kitchen table – like we do – and talk all about it?"

Ashley giggled as she tried to imagine her brothers chatting about their troubles over a cup of coffee and a caramel roll. "Goodness, no," she said on a sigh. "They'd never do that."

"But that's what you expected Mathew to do, isn't it?" Mrs. Holmes' voice was gentle as she made the point. Again she patted Ashley's hand and looked into her eyes. "He's worth the effort to get to know him better and he's worth every ounce of understanding you can muster."

Foolish pride and pettiness had driven Ashley out of the house where she could have seen Matt this morning, where she might have learned what caused his withdrawal from her presence last night. She'd fled and now recognized that she was disappointed in herself for not trusting him and for not trusting herself. "Thank you. Thank you for helping me see the situation more clearly."

"I have another concern, though," Ashley pressed on.

"What's that?"

"Matt has so much on his plate … with his sister missing, his mom's treatments, his business, and now his stepfather wanting back into their lives … I just don't want to add to his burdens," Ashley confessed.

Mrs. Holmes regarded her guest quietly for a moment before replying. "I doubt that you're a burden to anyone whose life you touch," she said. "You are strong and resilient, resourceful. You are far from being a burden."

"Matt's just got so many responsibilities – and I don't want to become someone else he feels he has to take care of …"

"I have a feeling the opposite is true," Mrs. Holmes countered. "I'd bet my '57 Chevy that you lighten his load – that you actually make it easier for Matt to take care of the responsibilities he has." The older woman paused before continuing, "In Proverbs, it says 'A joyful heart is good medicine,' and you are most definitely good medicine for Mathew."

Ashley raised an eyebrow in question, "It says that in the Bible? You're using quotes from the Bible to do matchmaking?"

"Yes," Mrs. Holmes responded without clarifying which question she was answering. "And, as a point of clarification, not every responsibility is a burden."

Hadn't she questioned God about how much Matt was to handle alone, only to feel that she was supposed to support and help him? And hadn't it frightened her to feel that way? Maybe it frightened Matt to let someone else into his life – to let someone help with the responsibilities he shouldered.

Ashley pushed the plate with the half-eaten roll toward the center of the table and took another sip of the coffee. She folded her hands and stared at them for a long time before lifting her gaze to meet the wise eyes of Mrs. Holmes. The silvery-gray eyes watched her with calm confidence. Finally, with a great sigh, Ashley said quietly, "I'm scared."

"Of what, dear? God's direction in your life?"

Shaking her head in denial, Ashley offered a quiet, “No. I’m afraid I’ll make a mistake. When I was alone, if I made a mistake, it only affected me. I *really* don’t want to cause Matt any pain.”

“Why would you?”

“I don’t know.”

“You said you don’t want to hurt Matt,” Mrs. Holmes stated. “But when you arrived at my doorstep this morning, you said you were thinking of leaving …”

“This is not what I had planned,” Ashley tried to explain. “I never imagined myself in a small town.”

“Is that it? The small town is the problem?” Mrs. Holmes asked. “Your best friends have found their ways to this community and are happy here, but that doesn’t mean that it’s for you,” she said thoughtfully. “But, just because you never imagined yourself here, doesn’t mean you won’t find fulfillment here.” The older woman watched Ashley intently, as if trying to figure out a puzzle before she asked, “Why did you think you need to leave? I think I missed your reasoning?”

“I’m afraid I will break his heart. And he’s already lost so much.” Silence followed the statement. Ashley had blurted the words without thinking to censor her thoughts and now, embarrassed, she rose and moved to look out the kitchen window.

“There is no fear in love; but perfect love casteth out fear ...” The response was clear and quick from Mrs. Holmes. “If you and Matt can grow to love each other, or if you already do love each other, that love can help bring peace. It can settle your fears … give you both stability and confidence that you’ve been missing.”

Mrs. Holmes regarded Ashley for a long moment before she added, “Running away won’t help either of you. And, I think, it will break *both* your hearts.”

CHAPTER SIXTEEN

After visiting with Mrs. Holmes, Ashley had called Matt's phone and left a message, saying she was sorry for leaving without talking to him, but she'd like to have lunch together if that would be alright. She'd showered and had breakfast, setting her mind on getting down to the business of learning the business from Charlie and Catherine. She could report the news, but she needed to acquire more information about the business side of owning a newspaper.

Ashley arrived at the Chronicle office a little after nine o'clock, primed for the day ahead. Since learning that she owned the Chronicle, Ashley's passion for journalism had been reignited. She had discovered that she thoroughly enjoyed the interview process and the crafting of the articles.

Ashley hadn't grown up in a small town. She hadn't lived in a small town. And she most definitely had never reported the news in a small town. Initially, she expected that writing for a community newspaper would make her feel worthless and disgruntled. But after weeks of reporting how much snow had fallen in recent days, writing a fluff piece about a man who collects marbles, another about the owner of the only seeing-eye-dog in a hundred mile radius, and rewriting submissions by school teachers, she felt as though she had a career that helped others – a career that really mattered to the community.

Weddings, anniversaries and open houses were easy to write. Photos of ribbon cuttings and check-passings were easy to take. No danger. No risk. No chance of more concussions. Ashley was surprised by how comfortable she was in the role as a news reporter/photographer for a thriving weekly newspaper on the frozen northern plains.

The realization, instead of spreading alarm through her system, left Ashley with a feeling of rightness and calmness. She was enjoying her job, enjoying the town and her friends, and Matt. Matt – why hadn't he responded to her message? Was he upset with her for leaving? For some other reason? Maybe he was just busy helping his mom. Maybe he'd had a relapse and needed help. Ashley discarded each concern as they popped into her mind. Matt would get back to her when he could, she knew with a growing confidence.

Ashley spent the morning poring over the ordering procedures, as well as becoming familiar with various vendors on which Catherine and Charlie had relied for decades. They discussed what happened in the days Ashley was helping Melanie and Matt. Catherine assured her that there had been no more "shenanigans" in the days since the furnace was damaged, however, the police had not discovered who had committed the vandalism or why.

As Ashley concentrated on setting up a new computerized bookkeeping program, she became aware that Neal had entered the room. His now familiar sneer appeared when she looked up. "Hi Neal," she greeted him pleasantly. "How can I help you?"

The sneer morphed into an honest to goodness smile before he replied, "You could leave again."

"Sorry, Neal," she replied. "That's not going to happen. Let's move forward, shall we?" Not wanting to grant him the opportunity to scan the bookkeeping, she stood and met him in a few steps as he entered the office. "What's on your mind?"

"Well, one of us needs to leave. I was hoping it would be you," he began as he pulled an envelope from his pocket. "But if you won't leave, then I will." He handed the envelope to Ashley. "My notice. And I'd thank you not to send the police after me again." He spun on his heel and strode away.

A sense of relief filled Ashley. Because he had resigned, she wouldn't have to deal with Neal's attitude or his laziness and lack of productivity. She would however, need to replace him with a new reporter. She stuffed the envelope into her pocket and turned her attention toward the bookkeeping program once again.

The next time she looked up, Matt leaned against the doorjamb, smiling as he watched her. Ashley couldn't help but return the smile as pleasure coursed through her – he had gotten her message. "Hi, handsome," she said. "I hope you haven't been there long …" She shut down the computer as she spoke. "Ready for lunch?" She dug for the office keys in her bag, while continuing nervously, "I'll just lock up and we can go."

"No need. Bobbie locked me in as she left for her lunch break," he informed her in a quiet tone. "Everybody is gone." Matt's smile hadn't wavered, and he pushed off from the framework. "I'm honored that you invited me to join you," he said as he smoothly covered the distance between them. Pulling her into a quick hug, he whispered, "You scared me this morning when I found you had left the house." Ashley welcomed the hug, pulling herself as close to Matt as she dared.

He eased her back without releasing her and when their gazes met, Ashley felt as though his pain was hers; his fears were hers; but also, his love and joy were hers as well. His hands slid from her back, to her arms, and on up her neck, raising goose bumps where they'd lingered. They came to rest on her neck, with his thumbs gently brushing her cheeks, and then he bent to kiss her slowly and sweetly. When the pair broke apart, he whispered, "I don't know if I could bear losing you."

"I'm sorry. I didn't mean to alarm you," Ashley said as she looked again into the bright crystal blue eyes of the man she'd grown to love. "It was agonizing when you told me to go away. I was bruised and confused. And I ran back to my apartment."

She saw rising apprehension in Matt's expression and instinctively moved to reassure him. "That's as far as I would ever run, Matt. I'm here to stay," she declared earnestly. "I cannot see myself leaving Miller's Bend – my future is here, my business is here, my friends are here and my heart is here … with you."

Cautious acceptance of her proclamation crossed Matt's features, and he relaxed a bit. "I'm sorry, I told you to go away last night," he said quietly. "I didn't mean *leave*. I meant I needed space and time to think."

Ashley smiled up at him and asked, "Could you maybe say what you mean next time, please?"

Nodding in response, he pulled her close. "I'll try to remember that." After a moment he suggested, "How about lunch?"

They left by the back door, securing the lock, before getting into Matt's Camaro. "How did you manage to get a car like this?" she asked as they pulled into traffic.

"I picked it up after it had been totaled and I rebuilt it," Matt answered. "Mom has a picture of my father and Byron by a car just like it when they were younger."

"They knew each other?" Ashley gaped.

"Yah, weird isn't it?" Matt replied. "I didn't know until Byron came to town recently, but they had been really close friends. Byron said my dad had made him promise to take care of us if anything ever happened to him. That's why Byron married Mom – not out of love."

"You don't know … they might have had love," Ashley speculated. "But even if they did, they still had grief, regrets, and probably guilt. It would have been a lot to deal with."

Matt stopped at a traffic light and looked at Ashley. "They didn't deal with it. He abandoned us and Mom took me and Chrissi and she ran." The light changed, and the pair traveled a few blocks farther before pulling into the American-Mexican fast food restaurant. He parked the car and turned, locking gazes with Ashley, he spoke carefully. "I think I love you, but please, don't ever do that to me. Don't ever run away."

She leaned toward him, touching her hand to his cheek before she spoke. "I don't see that happening," she offered in assurance. "But let's promise each other, that if we feel like there is a problem developing, we'll talk about it." He didn't respond, but tugged her closer for a quick kiss.

The buzz of his cell phone drew their attention, and he answered the incoming call. As he listened, Matt's expression transformed with irritation, his skin paling. He turned to face forward in his seat again, pulling at his seat belt to clip it back into place as he listened to the caller. "I'll be there in five minutes," he announced to the caller then glanced at Ashley and added, "Or maybe ten." He disconnected the call, dropping the phone into his pocket. As he turned the key in the ignition, he explained, "Sorry, but lunch just got postponed."

Ashley was clicking her seat belt into place as she asked, "What is it? Your mom?"

"No. Byron's with her. She's fine," he assured her as he backed from the parking space. "It's Chrissi." The pale tone of his skin had been replaced with the rich rosiness of anger.

"She's back … here in Miller's Bend, and didn't even call to let us know she was alive." Throwing the shift lever into Drive, he sent Ashley a dark look, and spoke quietly, "I'm going to kill her."

"You wouldn't!"

"No, I wouldn't," he confessed. "But, I'd like to scare her as much as she's scared us."

"I doubt that," Ashley countered calmly.

"I'll just drop you off …" he said absently but stopped without completing the sentence. Ashley was good for him … made him feel stable, confident. Maybe it would be good to have her along. Glancing toward her, he changed tacks, "She's at the police station. Would you want to come with me?"

She hesitated. "You're sure you want me along? I mean … it's a ... you might want to be alone with her … you know, so you can kill her without witnesses," she said with a smile.

"I'm sure," he confirmed. "I want you there, if you have the time."

"If you're sure … I'm glad to come along."

They pulled into a parking spot, and raced inside the police headquarters. Police Chief Jeff Schuster met them just inside the door. He nodded in greeting to Ashley, and then slapping a hand to Matt's shoulder, he spoke with a robust vigor, "Bet you were glad to get my call. Chrissi is right this way …" He guided Matt toward the interrogation room, but Ashley dropped back. She waited, uncertain what to do. She turned to study a map of the city which was drawn in the early 1900s. It had been tastefully framed and displayed in the lobby. She stepped closer to examine the names of the streets, when a hand closed around her upper arm. "Come on, Ash," Matt's voice reverberated close to her ear. "I need you with me, please."

Looking up into his eyes, she saw that his words rang with truth; he sincerely wanted her in the room with him and Chrissi. She nodded and stepped closer. With his arm wrapped around her shoulders they moved through the hall, and Matt pushed through the door into the interrogation room.

A young woman with a heavy black braid and sad blue eyes, with murky dark rings beneath them, lurched from one of the hard plastic chairs positioned around the dark table, running straight into Matt's embrace. He didn't release Ashley – just pulled her into the same encircling hug with his beloved sister. Chrissi, who had been as strong as she could be for weeks, collapsed against her brother's chest and let the love of family enfold her as she cried.

Ashley had pressed her arm around Chrissi in silent support. Maybe someday down the road, they would be sisters-in-law; maybe not, but Ashley sensed the girl needed comfort in this moment. Ashley peeked up to gauge Matt's state of mind and found tears in his eyes as he held tightly to his little sister. "Thank God you're home," he rasped, as he squeezed Chrissi even tighter.

The door opened abruptly, breaking the spell, and Mason surged into the room followed closely by Tyler. Ashley noted a wildness emanating from Tyler as he entered the room, but he reined it in quickly when he looked at the trio clutched in embrace. Matt released the women and clasped Mason's hand in a quick shake. He greeted him with quiet words, "Glad you could make it, buddy." And then glancing at Tyler, he cocked his head and lifted an eyebrow in an unspoken question.

Tyler grinned, and hooking a thumb toward the lawyer, he responded, "I was with Mason when the chief called."

Chief Schuster herded everyone toward the table, telling them gruffly that they should each take a seat. He settled himself at the head of the table and cleared his throat. "I just love a happy ending," he began. "Chrissi is back safe and sound, thanks to Agent Joseph Stockard, here," he commented with a wide smile and a gesture toward the man who had been seated at the table. And then, addressing the thin young woman, he added, "You'll be able to sleep in your own bed tonight, honey. You're mamma's going to be so happy."

A booming voice broke in. "Not so fast," Stockard interjected. "We've got a lot of information to cover here."

Matt's defenses flared. "She hasn't done anything wrong, has she?" he asked, as his focus intensified on the stranger who occupied the chair next to Chrissi. She didn't look up but, Ashley heard the young woman sniffle again.

"Nothing illegal," Stockard confirmed. "But she's in plenty of trouble … and it might even follow her here."

"No," Chrissi declared feebly. "I won't let it follow me."

"Where did you go? What were you doing?" Tyler broke in. "What were you thinking?!"

She looked up then, meeting Tyler's demanding glare. Her voice cracked, "I …"

Stockard stood and leaned across the table, blocking Chrissi from Tyler's view, while fixing a menacing stare on him. "And who are you? Why are you even in this room?" he demanded.

Standing, but much shorter than the other man, Tyler replied calmly, "I'm a friend of the family. I'm here for moral support." he paused and leaned so he could make eye contact with Chrissi and winked. "Besides," he added, "I like riding around with the attorneys … then I sell news tips to the local paper."

Stockard cast a dark look at those seated around the table before turning to Chief Schuster. "You're going to let him stay in here?" he demanded.

"Well, he's right. He's like a brother to Matt, and …" the chief replied, but let the words trail away as he glanced between Tyler and Chrissi. "'Sides that," he continued, "That 'un is my son. He's sat in on more interviews than Diane Sawyer."

Mason snorted, drawing Stockard's attention. "I suppose you are the -"

"Attorney for the family, Agent Stockard," Mason interjected. He stood as he extended his hand and added, "Mason Alexander. Pleased to meet you."

A sound of disgust came from deep within Stockard as he turned his attention back to the chief. "And who's the redhead? Brenda Starr?"

The chief's eyes widened and his face flushed – whether with anger or embarrassment, Ashley wasn't certain. "As a matter of fact -" he began to respond.

"She's with me," Matt asserted as Stockard focused his attention on the couple. "She stays."

"Why didn't you just call a town meeting?" the agent said with sarcasm. "That way there'd be no need for gossip."

"Pendleton," the chief called to an officer who was seated near the door. "Why don't you go get some coffee and a pitcher of water for us while we start over?"

"Yes, sir," came a quick reply and the young officer bolted from the room.

Stockard raked a hand through his hair as he asked, "Where's Sheriff Dunn? I've been working with him and now he's not even here …"

"Got called to a traffic incident out on Highway 212," the chief replied calmly. "He'll be along when he can get here." He shifted in his chair before suggesting, "Maybe you could bring us up to speed on what's happened."

He had Chrissi tell the first installment of the tale. She'd located her father through the internet when she was fifteen years old. She'd corresponded with him regularly and learned that she had two cousins, Maddy and Sierra. She'd become friends with them, and when she'd decided that Maddy was in serious trouble, she went to Chicago to try to find her and save her.

"Why did you go to Boulder first?" Matt inquired.

"I needed more money than I had access to. I went to Dad for it."

"Dad? Byron gave you money?!" Matt's voice rose drastically in volume, while dropping to a dangerous range. "Then he's responsible for all of this!" Matt railed. "I'll wring his neck!"

Ashley touched his arm gently, bringing him back to an emotional center. He glanced at her and felt calmness settle over him. "No, you won't," she said quietly, confidently.

"But without that money, she'd have had to come home," he countered.

"I wouldn't have," his spirited sister insisted. "I'd have gone, but it would have been more difficult." Matt swiveled to take in Chrissi's determined expression, and he knew she was right – nothing would have stopped her from the fool's mission she'd set for herself.

"And, if she hadn't gone to Byron first, he wouldn't have come to us," the chief pointed out. "Dunn contacted the officials in Chicago after we had information from Byron. Otherwise we would have had no idea where to look for Chrissi."

Stockard joined in the assessment again, saying, "If Dunn hadn't notified us, we would have arrested her as if she was just another drugged up hooker when we found her."

The room fell silent for a heartbeat. "Thanks a lot, Number Four," Chrissi said quietly, but with a benign twist of sarcasm.

In a scramble of fury, both Matt and Tyler lurched toward Stockard with murderous intent in their eyes. Mason grasped Tyler and dragged him back into his seat. The chief had pushed himself out of the chair sending it flying behind him, and yanked Stockard back and away from Matt's attack.

Muttering a quick oath, he jabbed a finger into Matt's chest, demanding, "Sit down! Right now!" Defiance glowed in Matt's features and his eyes sparked dangerously. "I swear, Mathew, if you touch that man you'll be in a federal pen faster than you can say 'parole'. Now sit down."

After a silent battle of wills, Matt regained some composure and complied. He looked intently at Chrissi, the little sister he had cherished and protected all of her life, and his heart wrenched. What had happened? Could it be that she'd changed that much in the weeks since she'd left Miller's Bend?

CHAPTER SEVENTEEN

(Readers, if you are sensitive to violence, please skip to Chapter 18, page 207.)

The room was too tightly constrained to contain the potentially explosive emotions of those present, Ashley thought as she watched the outward expression of rising antagonism between the men. Straightening as she rose from her chair, she cleared her throat, grappling for words that would calm them. "Gentlemen," she began, but before she could form the rest of her statement, the door was flung open.

The hinges creaked and the door handle crashed into the drywall. *That's going to leave a mark*, she thought distractedly. Ashley, like the others, had expected Pendleton to return bearing the requested refreshments, or perhaps, the arrival of Sheriff Dunn. But the man whose form filled the doorway was neither. An evil rage poured off of the man. As he raised his right arm, Ashley recognized that he held a semiautomatic handgun, which he was casting left and right as though searching for his target. "Oh, dear God," she whispered desperately. It would be like shooting ducks in a barrel.

Later Ashley would reflect that, as she'd learned more than once on assignment, at moments like these, time neither slows nor speeds, as is often depicted in works of fiction. Time simply goes on … one second, two seconds, three seconds, four and five.

The gun shots rang out, accompanied by screams, which Ashley's mind attributed to Chrissi, but she may have contributed a few of her own. She registered the yelling of orders, and cries of pain. Ashley lay still on the floor, eyes clenched tightly closed, praying and listening: gasping sobs, moans of torment, a frightening faint gurgling sound and Matt's whispered, "Are you okay?"

She cautiously uncovered her head and turned toward his voice and the feel of his breath against her cheek, and found Matt's intense gaze searching her features. She nodded, "I think so. Chrissi?" Even as she asked, Matt left her side and joined Tyler as he rushed instinctively toward the young woman, who lay partially concealed by an unmoving Agent Stockard.

Ashley's quick glance around the room accounted for everyone. Matt and Tyler were rolling Stockard off of Chrissi; Chief Schuster lay flat on his back beyond the table, service revolver in hand, moaning and gasping; Mason was tending to the chief, applying pressure to try to slow the flow of blood from the wound on his shoulder. Or was it his chest?

Ashley fumbled for her cell phone and began pushing in the 911 call, wondering who would respond when the Chief was down, Agent Stockard was down and Officer Pendleton ... Her glance swung from the chief and Mason to the doorway where the assailant had towered less than a minute earlier. Pendleton was on his knees performing CPR on the man who had been intent on killing … killing who? Which of them had been his target?

"911. What's your emergency?" the dispatcher inquired, breaking into Ashley's thoughts. *People are dying,* she thought.

“We need multiple ambulances at the Miller’s Bend police station,” Ashley said clearly. “Three gunshot victims.” She glanced around the room again. “There may be more injured. I can’t be sure yet.”

Ashley heard the keystrokes on what she assumed was a computer keyboard before the dispatcher spoke again. “Ambulances are en route. I’ll page the local police department as well. Ma’am, remain calm and stay on the line until they arrive.”

Stay calm?

“I am calm,” Ashley asserted defensively. Her eyes swept the room again, coming to rest on Jeff Schuster as his radio crackled with the page. “Sir?” she said into the phone. “You don’t need to page the police chief - he’s one of the wounded. Officer Pendleton is on the scene too, but you might get some backup in here.”

“Who else is there, Ma’am?” the voice asked.

“I don’t have time … I’ll leave the line open, but I’m putting the phone down,” Ashley replied.

Chrissi’s sobs reached a crescendo as her brother tried to comfort her. She backed away, scooting on the floor toward a wall. Her wild gaze bounced frantically from Matt to where Agent Stockard lay inertly with Tyler sitting on his knees next to the large man’s body, but doing nothing. “Help him!” Chrissi screeched. Tears streamed down her cheeks. “Help him, Ty!”

Tyler moved toward Chrissi, with a hand outstretched. “I can’t, Chris, I can’t” he replied brokenly. With Matt and Tyler both closing in on Chrissi, the girl’s agitation was rising as she began scooting backwards again, sliding along the wall toward a corner. Like a trapped animal.

She started to rise as she slid along the wall, hands bracing against the pale gray paint, smearing tears, makeup and blood from her hands in a trail. “You’re an EMT, Ty – you have to help him!” she wailed. “You have to!” Chrissi’s head was thrown back, eyes squeezed tightly closed, as she cried for the man who had saved her life back in Chicago.

Matt lurched to grab his sister, intending to hold her and comfort her, but she’s sensed the move and snapped back to attention. Terror rising in her eyes, she flattened her back into the corner. Ashley had seen the behavior before, when she’d been on assignment. Abused, traumatized - victimized - women behaved this way. The two men, who thought they were trying to comfort Chrissi, were actually spiking her fear.

“Matt. Tyler,” Ashley’s softer voice drew their attention. “Why don’t you see if you can help … the others? And I’ll talk to Chrissi?” Their attention shifted, and when Tyler saw his father sprawled on the floor, he ran to him.

Matt’s eyes filled with tears as his gaze followed his friend. “God help us,” he whispered as he watched Tyler, kneeling in his father’s blood, taking over the limited medical aid Mason had been administering. The chief was still alive, thanks to Mason’s efforts, but he was ghastly pale, his breathing shallow and skin beaded with perspiration.

Ashley lightly pushed Matt’s shoulder, encouraging him to move toward the others. “I’ve got Chrissi,” she said. “You help your friends.” Reluctantly, he stepped over to where the three men were on the floor. Matt placed a hand on Tyler’s shoulder in silent support. If Jeff Schuster died, Ty would lose his father – his entire family, and Matt would lose the closest thing to a father he’d had in 16 years. Shared grief bonded the men, although they said nothing.

The younger woman allowed Ashley to wrap her in an embrace, and let out a shaky sigh as the men stepped back. Remorse moved through her features as she knew it had injured them when she couldn't accept their attention. A shiver slithered down her spine when Chrissi glanced toward the doorway. The former Eagle Scout Josh Pendleton was trying his best to save the life of that disgusting, vile, murderous lowlife – Slug. Chrissi tried to pull away from Ashley as she felt the bile rise, but the woman held her even as she dropped to her knees and vomited violently.

Uniformed EMTs burst into the room, and to their credit, they didn't flinch at the scene that met them. Mason had moved silently to Agent Stockard's side, already suspecting the reason that Tyler hadn't stayed with him, but needing to check for himself. It was readily evident that he had taken more than one bullet in an attempt to protect Chrissi from the gunman. One had caught him in the neck, killing him.

As the first set of EMTs prepared the assailant to be transported, the second crew stepped past him carrying equipment to Schuster's position. An older EMT nudged Tyler saying, "Come on, son. Let us work."

Tyler looked up into the face of the man towering over them and saw confidence and professionalism. Even though the patient was a long-time friend, the man had blocked out his emotions – he had a job to do. Tyler nodded and started to stand, but his father's lips began to move. "Ty?"

"Yah, Dad, I'm here," he choked.

"Love you," the older man whispered without opening his eyes. He swallowed hard, and added in a dry, rasping voice. "I'm so sorry."

He said no more, and the EMT pushed Tyler again. "We have to move," he said.

CHAPTER EIGHTEEN

Accompanied by Byron, Melanie had rushed to Chrissi's hospital bedside. Chrissi's mother stayed as long as she dared, but when she could no longer hide her increasing fatigue, Byron insisted on taking her home again. In the wake of the shooting, Matt stayed at the hospital so he could check on Chrissi frequently. He also worried and prayed over Jeff Schuster, who was still fighting for his life. The man had been a surrogate father to Matt since he, Tyler and Riley had become friends so many years ago. Jeff and Tyler formed a small, loving family unit, with only each other to rely on, and Matt wanted to be there for them.

Matt dozed lightly, but jerked awake when he felt a light touch on his arm. He scrambled upright in the hospital waiting room chair. He rubbed his eyes with the thumb and forefinger of his right hand as his left gently grasped the hand that had touched him. Looking up, he saw the exhausted, but loving, face of Ashley. "You didn't need to come back," he said in a rough, low voice. He tried to pull her closer, but she pulled against him, encouraging him to stand.

A quick glanced confirmed that Matt and Ashley were alone in the small area designated for families and visitors who needed to linger in the hospital. Nurses, staff and volunteers flashed past the open door periodically, but no one peeked inside as they passed. Beepers, buzzers, phones, and voices over the intercom interplayed with the other sounds that were typical of a hospital.

"I knew you'd say that," she confirmed as she stepped forward, and wrapped her arms around his waist. Matt let out a shaky sigh and held her tightly letting his chin rest on the top of her head, as Ashley continued, "I tried, but I couldn't stay away."

Hours had passed since the shooting - the horrifyingly gruesome shooting. All of those present had been taken to the hospital – except for Agent Stockard, of course. His body had been transported to the funeral home, Matt supposed, to be prepared for the trip to his home, where his family would grieve.

After being thoroughly evaluated for injuries, each had been taken to a conference room, where they spoke with ranking local police officers, Sheriff Dunn and investigators from the State Department of Criminal Investigation. When they had finished interviewing Ashley, she had confidentially told Matt that she would head back to the office of the Chronicle, to check on things and to draft a news story about the day's events. He suspected that her ulterior motive was to allow him time alone with his family members and friends who were dealing with the trauma.

"I'm so glad you are here with me. Thanks for coming back," Matt replied belatedly. Without speaking, they held each other for several minutes, drawing strength, giving comfort. He reflected on how he had grown to love the woman in his arms, and silently thanked God for letting them find each other. He was a romantic and well aware that he'd longed for the right woman to love, honor and cherish for the rest of his life. The certainty that she was in his embrace washed over him.

They would have to wait, of course. Chrissi had been admitted to the hospital and sedated. He wouldn't want to go on with his life, while his sister struggled to get her own life back to normal. And then there was their mother – her medical needs, and emotional needs, were his responsibility.

He was still working unreasonable hours trying to establish himself in the art world with the goal of making a solid living so he could support a wife and a family. Byron had reappeared and was causing ripples in Matt's life, in his heart and in his conscience. He had a lot of things to work through before he could move forward with what he wanted.

He squeezed Ashley a little tighter. When would he be able to put his own wants first? How could he ask Ashley to marry him, but ask her to wait for everything else in his life to settle down first?

Ashley wriggled a little away from Matt's chest and looked up, catching his troubled expression. "What's bothering you?" she asked. And then with blatant embarrassment, she continued, "I mean besides the obvious – today's events? You seem absorbed in some inner turmoil."

His heart pumped fast as he held back the words, "Marry me?" Instead, he slid his right hand up the smooth back of the intriguing woman and slipped it around to cup her cheek gently. "I love you," he said simply, before he bent his head to deliver a kiss that expressed quietly and respectfully the truth of the statement.

When he released Ashley, she stepped back and turned nervously away. Matt's confidence evaporated as he watched her shoulders rise on a deep intake of air and drop again as she sighed. She turned to face him with uncertainty in her expression. And, he noted sadly, she hadn't said that she loved him.

With the cautious steps of a tightrope walker, she moved closer again, stopping near enough that he could reach out and touch her if Matt felt compelled to do so. But her guarded expression held him frozen. "I remembered more," she whispered. "I know why I left my job – why I bought the Chronicle – why I wanted to be here. I thought I would be living in a quiet little town, where horrible things don't happen in a matter of seconds."

Matt found his voice. "But events like today's can happen any place," he said with resignation. "That's what you learned today, right?"

"Well, yes. They can," Ashley replied. "But that's not the lesson I'm taking away from today's tragedy."

She reached for his hand, held it, squeezing tightly. And when her gaze captured his again, tears stood in her eyes. "Today I learned how much easier it is to cope with emergencies and traumas when you are surrounded by friends and people who love you."

"No one is through coping with this," Matt countered. "There will be weeks and months of repercussions. It'll still be hard." He thought of Jeff Schuster who lay in the ICU unit fighting for his life. And of the chief's son, Tyler, who had fled the hospital in response to the emotional cascade. He sympathized with young police officer, Pendleton, who had kept the assailant alive until the EMTs arrived, only to learn that he died later in surgery. He prayed for them all, including Agent Stockard, who had given his life protecting Chrissi.

And he prayed for Chrissi. His heart ached for his baby sister, who had grown up, thinking she could save the world. She'd gone off, learned hard lessons and returned emotionally battered and bruised, only to be further traumatized by today's events. "It's going to be very hard," he repeated to himself.

Ashley drew his attention again. "So …" she began. "I don't know the answers – I'm not sure what's right with any degree of certainty. But I know I can't protect myself simply by living here. Bad things can still happen, even in a quiet little town like Miller's Bend."

The old fear of being left began to claw its way to the surface as Matt listened. Was she laying the foundation for an "I'm leaving" speech? Apprehensively, he waited, as she continued, "We don't know what's going to happen. Or when or where tragedies will strike -"

"Ashley, don't," he half warned, half pleaded.

With a furrowed brow, she cocked her head to one side slightly. "Don't what?"

Don't hurt me. Don't leave.

"Don't …" Matt paused, wondering what to say without being openly vulnerable.

"Matt. Please don't get ahead of me," she beseeched. "Just hear me out."

The pounding of his pulse in Matt's ears made it hard to concentrate. Panic flared and protective instincts urged him to retreat, but he stood stoically. After the day they'd had, she wouldn't dare push him away, would she?

"You don't know how much I appreciated you being there today. With me," he blurted without thinking. "It was a horrible experience, but you helped more than I can explain. Especially with Chrissi." His gaze held Ashley's, and when she would have spoken, he raised a hand, asking her to wait. "It's hard for me to admit when I need help. Assistance. But I thank God that you're in my life."

She stepped closer, and opened her mouth intent on speaking. But Matt pulled her closer and kissed her with desperation. The physical attraction between them was undeniable, but their hearts, spirits, indeed their whole beings longed to be together. When they separated, just enough for propriety's sake, Ashley's confidence blossomed. She knew that the path she'd set out to suggest would be the right one. But before she could speak, Matt clutched her close to his heart. With lips near her ear, he whispered, "Don't leave me."

"Leave?" She echoed. And then, looking up into his eyes, she read a rainbow of emotions – love, admiration, fear, apprehension – and she was moved to relieve his anxiety, she felt the need to calm his disquiet. And, although her spirit ached to shout from the rooftop, she spoke with quiet reverence, "I don't ever want to leave you, Mathew Vander Meer, champion of damsels." She stretched up on her tip toes, leaning into his body again. His hands trembled slightly as they went instinctively to her waist, to balance her, to pull her close. He'd bent forward, lowering his head, curling toward her. After a heartbeat, she whispered in his ear, "I want to marry you."

Matt's hold on Ashley tightened as he digested her words, her message. She wanted to marry him and he wanted nothing in this world more than to marry her. His mind raced ahead to a time when he hoped his mother's cancer would be in remission, and Chrissi would be back to her old self. In the spring … they could marry in the spring or maybe summer.

His throat was tight when Matt replied. "I want to marry you, too. I love you so much." He kissed her again, fighting the urge to let his hands roam. Spring was a long time away.

A moment later, they sat in adjacent chairs, and Ashley leaned contentedly against the front of Matt's shoulder, while his arm wrapped around her shoulders. Each basked in the new-found knowledge that the other loved them deeply and enduringly. Eventually Matt ventured to ask, "Do you want to go with me to pick out your engagement ring?"

Ashley's red hair danced against Matt's chest as she shook her head slightly. "Don't need to." She raised her gaze to his and concluded, "I trust you to pick out the one that's right for me."

He pulled back, a look of mock horror in his expression, before speaking. "You can't be serious! You'll probably be disappointed," he warned. "I might pick out something ugly – and big enough to go on my own finger. You'd better come along." He paused as his expression turned pleading. "We could go to Sioux Falls, Fargo or even St. Cloud this weekend and buy the masterpiece you deserve."

"Umm. I was thinking we could actually get married this weekend," she said quietly. "What do you think?" Ashley stiffened and drew back when she felt and heard Matt's deep rumble of laughter. "What's so funny?" she demanded indignantly.

"You are, my love," came the kind reply. "As much as I'd like to have you as my wife that soon, I just don't think it's possible to pull a wedding together that fast. How about June? We could have an outdoor service."

He was laughing, and Ashley didn't see what part of her plan was funny. The man clearly didn't understand her sense of urgency. She stood and turned, facing Matt, hands braced on her hips, ready to make her point as clear to him as it was to her. Ashley Nelson was woman of action and she was about to make certain that Mr. Vander Meer understood that once she'd made a decision, she would act on it. Quickly.

The laughter died on his lips, and he sat up straighter, becoming somber, he said with mild disbelief, “You’re serious? I mean about the timing.”

An assertive nod of her head set her hair to bouncing, and the sight made Matt smile again. The coming months – no, years – were going to be fun. The thought made the smile he wore stretch even wider. She was serious, alright. He stretched a hand forward in invitation, and softness touched his expression. “I just thought,” he began to explain, “that a summer wedding would give us more time to enjoy dating -”

“Married people go on dates,” she interjected staunchly.

“Sure enough. They do,” he conceded with an endearing smile. “And we will, too.”

“Okay. That’s good,” she confirmed with another pert nod.

“I thought if we wait a while before we get hitched, Mom will be through with her treatments, maybe Byron will have … I don’t know … either have left or something, and Chrissi’s life would be back to normal. Jeff Schuster isn’t out of danger yet and Tyler’s all messed up over it.”

“Listen to yourself, Matt,” she spouted with increasing steam. “Who’s getting married anyhow? You and me? Or Tyler, his dad, your step-dad, your mom and your sister?”

“What do you mean?” Matt asked, as he rose to his feet. “I’m just being considerate. Besides, you can’t get married in less than a week. We’d have to get a license and, and, talk to the pastor. We’d have to see if the church is available … find a caterer … I don’t even know all the things we’d have to do. There’s no way. Is there?”

His expression was cautiously hopeful. Did he really want to rush the ceremony?

"Oh, Matt," she responded as she stepped nearer. "We need the pastor and we need our family and friends present, beyond that … well, the other stuff just doesn't matter."

"You're sure? You wouldn't feel like you missed out?" he asked earnestly. "I thought women dreamed about their wedding days for years. I thought everything would have to be perfect." His gaze searched her face for unspoken messages. She smiled, somewhat shyly, shaking her head.

"I'd rather miss out on the spectacle and have more time together with you, than waste time and energy on orchestrating a show for the town and delay the start of our life together," she declared kindly. She moved closer to him as she spoke, and now he was reaching for her again.

"You're sure?" he asked again. Concern shown in his expression as his gaze locked on hers. "I don't want to rush this. I don't want to ruin it somehow. Or jinx it," he confessed.

Ashley wished for the words that would erase signs of lingering concern in Matt's mind. "Trust your heart, Matt. Remember when we talked about the night on the patio? The night when I fell?"

She watched as Matt nodded, and then answered, "I remember. I was afraid you were seriously hurt."

"We had an instant connection, Matt," she said. "Remember when we talked? You said you'd been hoping for a real relationship with Lauren, but she broke up with you. She was leaving town. And you weren't upset, because you knew she wasn't the one for you."

"Right," he confirmed. Thinking of the one-sided conversation he'd been having with God, just before he realized someone was behind him, in the shadow of the building.

"You said you were asking God when you would find someone to love, and He dropped me there in front of you," she explained. "Is it possible that it was as simple as that? I was meant to find you, when I was searching for a safe, stable place to land?"

Matt paced away a few steps away and stopped. A question niggled at the back of his mind. A question he hadn't wanted to address, but he needed to. He didn't dare face Ashley as he asked, so standing with is back to her, feet spread, hands braced on his hips, he tipped his head back to stare at the line where the white wall of the waiting room met the white wall of the ceiling. "Are you sure it is you, Ashley, that I fell in love with? Or did I just fall in love with the first unsuspecting woman to come along?"

He heard some indignation, mixed with humor, in her reply. "In the first place – I am not unsuspecting. I am educated and successful and I've been all over the globe. I'm not given to fancy and fairy tales," she declared. "However," her voice softened and he heard her moving closer behind him. "I do recognize a blessing in my life when I see one. And Matt, you are the greatest blessing God has brought into my life in a long time."

His pulse was pounding loudly in his ears, as he turned to look into the face of the woman he'd loved almost from their first meeting. "You don't worry that I just transferred feelings for Lauren to you? That I would have latched onto anyone who happened into my path that night?"

A radiant smile broke across Ashley's expression. Filled with confidence, she closed the space between them, reaching again for Matt's hand. "You didn't love Lauren. You wanted to, but you didn't," she said quietly. "If you had, you wouldn't have let her leave you out there on the patio. You wouldn't have let her leave Miller's Bend without knowing how you felt. If you had loved her, Lauren would still be in your heart and there wouldn't have been room for you to let me in." She touched his cheek gently before adding, "Trust yourself, Matt. Trust your feelings."

He pulled her against his body for another embrace, and as he held her, he silently thanked God for Ashley's patience and wisdom. Matt was a lucky man, and he knew it. Ashley loved him and accepted his love for her. With a few short sentences, she had erased his self-doubt and reinforced his conviction that they were meant to be together.

"It's truly miraculous, isn't it? The way God puts us in proximity with hundreds or thousands of people, but opens our hearts to the possibility of deeply loving only a few precious souls?" she whispered against his chest. "You are precious to me and I want to be married to you as soon as possible.

"You really are amazing. You know that?"

"No. I just trust in God's guidance. I've learned from my life experiences, and also from stories of others, that time shouldn't be wasted," she said quietly.

"Others?"

"Mrs. Holmes, for example," Ashley answered. "Did you know that she made decisions that kept her from marrying her first love? And then circumstances eliminated the option completely."

"What happened?" Matt asked. "I've known her for years, but I didn't know that Harold wasn't who she would have wanted to marry. I've always heard that they had a good life together until he died."

Ashley shook her head. "Her story isn't mine to tell, at least not yet," she said, thinking of her conversations with Mrs. Holmes and the story she was writing but didn't have permission to publish. "The lesson is that we should accept the good things and people that God puts into our lives. Take them with love and appreciation; don't wait for something better or for a better time."

"Makes sense. Mostly," he acknowledged. Matt couldn't believe that he was actually considering a rushed wedding. If they pulled it off, people would talk. Some would be watching Ashley's sleek form for signs of a baby bump. The thought startled Matt with the image generated in his mind. A baby. The idea had loads of appeal.

The words slipped out before he thought to sensor them, "You want children?" And then he held his breath as he waited for her reply. He'd longed for a complete, proper family most of his life. If Ashley's visions of family didn't meld with his, what would they do?

Her sly smile conveyed the response before she formed the words, "Oh, yes. I want your children."

CHAPTER NINETEEN

The women had pulled it off, Matt reflected as he sat alone watching them working in the kitchen in the church's fellowship hall. Ashley, her mother, and her friends had planned the wedding in record time. They hadn't accomplished it in three days, as Ashley had hoped, but they were well inside the three week mark.

The ceremony had been conducted by their pastor just a short time ago. It was a typical exchange of wedding vows, but as Matt had spoken the words, he'd felt his spirit soar. He finally, finally felt the confidence that resulted from having Ashley's steadfast love. He realized that he'd been envious of his friends, Riley and Andrew, as he'd seen their relationships blossom with Shelby and Allison. But now he was joining their ranks – the ranks of the happily married men.

As he watched the women fussing in the kitchen, Matt searched for Chrissi among them. She wasn't there. He frowned. Chrissi had been acting strangely since her return and the trauma of the shooting. She'd only been hospitalized overnight after the tragedy. But upon her return home, she'd become moody and reclusive. He wondered what was going on with her, and had asked her several times over the weeks. "Nothing," was her standard reply.

Now his gaze roamed the fellowship hall until he spotted Chrissi sitting with her back to the rest of the room. She leaned forward in her chair as if in close conversation with a confidant. She shifted a little to one side and Matt saw a darkly clothed shoulder beyond hers. Who was sitting with her?

Matt started to rise, thinking he'd stroll over that way and casually check on his sister. Suddenly loud clatter and exclamations from the kitchen drew everyone's attention, and Chrissi turned toward the sounds. The move exposed the man with whom she huddled so intimately – Tyler! Matt read deep misery in his friend's silver eyes. Tyler held his gaze only a few seconds before the expression of pain morphed into something else – embarrassment perhaps – but then he closed off his expression. Almost defiantly, Tyler stood and guided Chrissi away from the rest of the group. They slipped into the hallway leading to the sanctuary and several other rooms.

When Matt would have moved to follow, a hand clapped firmly on his shoulder, causing him to pause. Carefully hiding the irritation at being sidetracked, Matt turned to face yet another well-wisher, and found his stepfather. Happiness radiated from the older man as they clasped hands in a firm shake. "Congratulations, again, Mathew," he said. "Your mother and I couldn't be happier for you."

Matt nodded in response, thankful that his beautiful bride was approaching with his mother. Melanie reached for her son, and Matt gladly pulled her in for a hug. "How are you holding up?" he asked with deep concern evident in the tone of his voice. "You're not overdoing things are you?"

With tears shimmering in her eyes, Melanie responded, "This is one of the happiest days of my life, and I hope it's the happiest day of your life, so far."

"It is," he confirmed, even as he reached to pull his new wife close to his side. "It absolutely is." Matt and Ashley's gazes had latched onto each other, the love coursing between the two. And he realized again just how blessed he was to have the love of such a woman. The future lay before them and he was eager to begin the journey.

The sound of Melanie's amused voice broke into his reverie. "We've got news," she began with an expansive, if somewhat tired, smile. Byron supported Melanie solicitously as she spoke. "Byron has decided to stay in Miller's Bend." She smiled up at her former husband, as she continued, "He's going to help me through the rest of my treatments. And then we might decide to try dating … see if things work out this time."

The news should have distressed Matt, but instead, he was instantly glad to know that Byron would be around. The two men had endured several conversations in recent weeks; the scars from the past had begun to heal. He'd realized that Byron and his mother each harbored feelings for the other, and surprisingly, Matt was happy for them. He nodded, "Sounds good."

"There's more," Byron interceded. "Your mother and I have a gift for the two of you."

"I've deeded the house to you and Ashley as a wedding gift," Melanie informed them with joy. "It'll be the perfect starter home for a young family."

"Thank you, Mrs. Gibson," Ashley said quietly. "That's very kind of you."

Matt cut in, "Too kind. Mom, you can't give us your house." He glanced to Byron for backup, but the man remained silent.

"It's what I want, Matt. I've taken an apartment," she explained. Pausing, she looked to Byron, before continuing, "In the same building that Byron's is in. He'll be close by to help me if I need anything."

"What's Chrissi supposed to do?" Matt asked sharply, but then caught himself. "She can stay with us, of course."

"No. You're newlyweds," Melanie countered. "We've made arrangements with Mrs. Holmes. Chrissi will be living in the apartment there."

So they had everything arranged … it was all taken care of. Matt had been letting go of his sense of responsibility for everyone in his life. Chrissi had been rebelling against anyone controlling her for several months. It seemed she had been having difficulties in finding her equilibrium since her return from Chicago, and maybe having her own space, and a sense of autonomy, would help. They would all be there for Chrissi, but maybe flexing her independence would allow her to grow and move forward.

"The house is a generous gift, Mom. I … we appreciate it very much. Thank you," he said with a gravelly voice. The gift of the freedom to focus on Ashley and their new life together was even greater, and one for which he couldn't voice his gratitude. But he was sure his mother understood.

"You deserve it, sweetheart," she said. "You deserve it."

CHAPTER TWENTY

While Ashley and Matt enjoyed a brief honeymoon, Shelby filled in as the reporter for the newspaper, and Catherine and Charlie continued to run the business. Upon their return, Ashley turned her attention and energies to running the newspaper, and soon discovered she needed help. Neal had left the same day that he'd handed Ashley his notice and hadn't been heard from since. The sense of relief Ashley felt at his absence almost sparked guilt in her conscience. However, he hadn't been a model employee, she would remind herself. The "shenanigans" had ended when he'd left the county, so Ashley and Sheriff Dunn concluded that Neal had been responsible after all.

Acknowledging that she couldn't handle all the news reporting and photography assignments alone, Ashley approached Shelby about working in the thriving news industry of Miller's Bend, and Shelby gladly accepted the offer. The two friends even discussed the possibility of becoming business partners.

With a happy heart and others to help share his responsibilities, Matt had thrown himself into his sculpting since their return from the honeymoon. When he stayed long hours at his studio, Ashley would sometimes visit with Mrs. Holmes for a while and then would return home and record her notes. She'd spent every spare moment crafting the old woman's story – everything she'd been told in the time they'd spent together. It included Mrs. Holmes' childhood, her choice to leave Miller's Bend, her lost love and hardships while she was away. The story swelled with love and hope as the young professional woman had returned to her hometown and married another. The years that MaryAnn and Harold toiled together to make their home what they'd wanted were included, as was the heartache of learning she would never bear him any children. Ashley had cried as she composed the account of Harold's untimely death and Mrs. Holmes' anguish.

In later years, the woman, who apparently had mentored much of the population of Miller's Bend at one time or another, had found her inner store of strength and once again became the strong, independent woman of her youth. Ashley had included the story Matt related to her about the time he, Riley and Tyler vandalized the wall of the garage belonging to Mrs. Holmes and how that had been the beginning of a friendship that bound the three men, then boys, to her in a unique sort of family. The bonds strengthened over the years since and each of the trio often checked in on the sweet old lady.

Ashley's story also emphasized the outreach provided to young, sometimes lost, adults who needed temporary housing. The way she let them into her home, renting out the basement apartment but rarely taking any reimbursement, was truly a sampling of God's work by mission. Ashley had composed the story and wanted to ask Shelby and Allison both to review it before she faced Mrs. Holmes with her idea. But a deep sense of needing to protect the woman's privacy held her back.

The events since Allison and Andrew's wedding had caused many changes, and as she stood on the doorstep of Mrs. Holmes' house, waiting for the woman to answer her knock, Ashley wondered if she should delay her request. Maybe the timing wasn't right. She recalled the way Mrs. Holmes had quickly dismissed Ashley's suggestion that she could write a story about her for the local newspaper. But Ashley had begun to write heedless of the woman's words.

And now, Ashley stood in the late-winter sunshine, wondering if she'd made a mistake. She had felt driven to record Mrs. Holmes' story – no, it hadn't been a mistake. What happened to the manuscript from this point forward would be up to the subject herself, though. Ashley had decided that she would not publish it without Mrs. Holmes' blessing and written consent.

The door opened a few inches, and then was thrown wide as Mrs. Holmes recognized her visitor. "Come in, come in," she welcomed warmly. "I'm so glad you stopped by. I've got fresh cookies baked and do you think any of my boys would show up?"

Ashley had learned that when Mrs. Holmes spoke of her boys, she meant Riley, Tyler and Matt, and sometimes Andrew, who had been "adopted" later in life than the others. Ashley smiled in response to the good-natured complaint, as she knew the woman received plenty of visitors. "Are you sure you have time to serve cookies? I know you are always busy …" Ashley protested mildly.

"Cookies and … I think we'll have ice cream with them today," Mrs. Holmes said cheerily. "I'm feeling like it's a special occasion." Ashley shed her coat and followed her hostess into the kitchen where a plate of chocolate chip cookies awaited.

"Are you sure so many sweets are good for you, Mrs. Holmes?" Ashley inquired. "We'd hate to damage your health and lose you."

"Oh, no worries," the old woman responded as she pulled a carton of ice cream from the freezer. "I will die one day, but I won't be lost." Ashley picked the scoop from the silverware drawer and did the honors of giving them each a modest curl of ice cream in a small bowl. As she returned the package to the freezer, Mrs. Holmes crushed her cookie and sprinkled it over the frozen treat.

The two enjoyed the snack and chatted over a variety of topics. Ashley was surprised to learn that Tyler had been a frequent visitor to the house, sometimes seeing the owner, and sometimes checking on the downstairs renter – Matt's sister, Chrissi. "Kind of reminds me of Riley," Mrs. Holmes commented. "Back when he would stop in to see if I needed anything, but he'd always be asking after Miss Shelby … Was she okay? Did she need for anything? Then he started going to her door more and more," she said with a sly smile. "And my door less and less."

Not knowing exactly how to respond to that bit of information, Ashley took a big bite of her ice cream and waited. She didn't wait long before Mrs. Holmes was informing her that she had attended the Frosty Festival at the preschool where Allison's daughter, Hope, was a student. Ashley was surprised to learn that the surrogate grandmother had also braved the subzero temperatures to watch Rori compete in a junior high gymnastics meet. "Should you be going out so much?" she asked with concern. "You could fall or get sick."

"I could fall or get sick here at home, too," Mrs. Holmes countered as her silver-grey eyes lit with amusement. "I'm going to live until I'm done living," she added determinedly. "I don't want to sit around and wither away."

And then changing the subject the hostess declared, "Your writing's getting better."

"What?"

"I read that newspaper from stem to stern every week. And, as I said, your writing is getting better," Mrs. Holmes responded.

Ashley was caught off guard by the quick change in conversation and by the comment. She laughed lightly, as she asked, "What was wrong with my writing?"

"Nothing in particular," Mrs. Holmes said as she rested a hand on Ashley's. "It's just getting better."

"Well … thank you … I think," the younger woman answered. It seemed like a good spot in the conversation to introduce the idea which had brought Ashley to Mrs. Holmes' home.

"Do you remember all the conversations you and I have had?" she began tentatively.

A smile lit the weathered face of the hostess. "My goodness, no. I don't remember them all," she paused. "But I have *enjoyed* them all."

Ashley rubbed nervously on the old woman's frail wrist. She didn't look into the face of her victim – hostess. "Well I've enjoyed them, too. And I didn't want to forget them, so I made notes. And then I … well, I organized the notes," she stammered. "I … um …" Ashley's voice trailed away. Why was it so hard to say?

"What is it girl? Say what's on your mind."

Ashley sat up straighter and looked directly into those beautiful, wise, caring eyes with the strange silver-gray color and she smiled. "I think I've grown to love you Mrs. Holmes, and I hope you aren't angry or upset, but I've written your story and I'd like your permission to have it published," Ashley said quietly to Mrs. Holmes. When the older woman didn't respond immediately, Ashley felt even more nervous and unsure of herself. "I know it was presumptuous of me to go ahead and write it without asking you first, but I hoped that when you see it, you will understand that I'm trying to honor you – your life and your faith. Your wisdom," she rambled. "Please, just consider it?"

"I'll consider it when it's complete," Mrs. Holmes said at length.

Confused, Ashley replied, "It may need some edits, but it's finished."

"It can't be finished. There are events you don't know *anything* about – people you don't know *everything* about," she explained. "Like my grandchild who lives here in Miller's Bend and doesn't even know me for who I am." Tears coursed over the paper-thin skin of her cheeks. "He doesn't know how much I love him, or that I would do anything to help him."

LOOK FOR
TAKING CARE
TYLER AND CHRISSI'S STORY,
COMING SOON!

Cadee Brystal's next novel is also set in Miller's Bend, where you've already met and grown to love the characters. Circumstances lead Tyler to reveal his feelings for Chrissi as he steps in to help her, even as he deals with a potentially devastating secret in his past. Tyler learns that fatherhood has more to do with the heart than with genetics.

www.ingramcontent.com/pod-product-compliance
Lightning Source LLC
Chambersburg PA
CBHW031724170626
46808CB00005B/1872
9780991441747